Second Chance at Love®

LET PASSION SOAR
SHERRY CARR

D0057945

A
SECOND CHANCE AT LOVE
BOOK

To Edith,

Thank you, Gemini, for your encouragement, knowledge, and patience in showing me the way and for your unfailing faith while I struggled to get here.

1

"YOU WANTED TO see me, Kacie?" Bob Gaines surveyed her with barely concealed irritation.

Kacie noted her boss's expression without any outward show of the annoyance she felt. She was well aware of her unpopularity in the firm—and of its causes. Even though she'd graduated with honors and received her master's in computer science, she was constantly subjected to—and required to ignore—sex prejudice in a predominantly male occupation. And never more so than here at Weston Technology. It was no secret that she had been hired away from Comco, her previous employer, with a big boost in salary and no loss of seniority. She supposed it was inevitable that resentment and bias from the men in her department would dog her footsteps.

She knew her looks and age were also strikes against her. Being twenty-eight, slim, with wavy blue-black, waist-length hair, an ivory complexion that steadfastly refused to tan no matter how hard she tried, and indigo eyes framed by thick, sooty lashes, was a definite disadvantage in her professional circle. While she didn't play up her physical assets, she didn't consciously hide them, either. Most of the time she was simply too busy to bother one way or the other.

"It's this new project," she explained, coming over to take the single chair across the desk from Bob. She placed a small stack of papers on the cluttered walnut desk top. "It's not going to work this way." She tapped the end result of her calculations with a long, pink-tipped finger. "I've revamped the first section."

"Hold it." Bob's command was abrupt. "Do you have any idea what you're talking about? This is the big boss's plan. Believe me, what he doesn't know about computers isn't worth knowing."

Kacie's temper escalated slightly, but her voice remained level. "Just look at the revisions, Bob. You can see for yourself."

He glared at her, obviously wanting to tell her to get out but knowing he at least had to go through the motions of scanning her proposal. "All right," he agreed grudgingly. "I'll check it over after lunch."

She nodded at his acceptance, not caring how reluctantly he gave it. She knew she was right about her figures. He would be a fool to ignore her changes, and he definitely wasn't that.

Kacie left his office and headed for the first-floor cafeteria. Because she'd been up late the night before, carefully reviewing her findings, she had overslept this morning, missing breakfast in her effort to get to work on time. As she joined the line, behind two secretaries she recognized as being from upper-level management, she vaguely wished she'd chosen to go out to eat.

Thus far, she had few friends in the company, so she frequently made lunch a solo venture. She eyed the two chattering girls in front of her with a momentary stab of envy.

"I tell you he's on his way to Atlanta, Stell."

The girl closer to Kacie looked skeptical. "You're crazy, Jean. Jake Weston has better things to do than to come down here," she drawled. "Didn't you hear about that Chicago merger?"

"I did. That's why he's coming. I can't wait to see him. I caught a glimpse of him the last time he was here. I had dreams about him for a week." She sighed dramatically, leaving her listeners in no doubt as to the kind of nightly visions she'd had.

"Don't waste your time, girl," her friend remarked as they approached the cashier. "He's been married before. Stands to reason that if he divorced one wife and never remarried, he sure isn't interested in another. He's wedded to the company, so I hear."

Kacie paid her tab and trailed the girls to the only remaining empty table in the room. She should have known better than to take the early lunch hour. It was always more crowded than any other. She couldn't avoid overhearing the rest of their conversation. To her surprise she found that she was actually curious about what they had to say.

She knew the Jake Weston success story, of course. Who in the company—or the entire computer business, for that matter—didn't? In his late thirties, he'd already achieved what few men hope to accomplish in a lifetime. Literally climbing from the streets, he'd won an athletic scholarship to college. Sheer determination got him through a year earlier than the usual four. A short stint with a crumbling computer firm, which he later bought, was the beginning of his financial empire. He had offices in his native New York, one here, and now one in Chicago.

It was this new acquisition that was a source of personal irritation for Kacie. It was his organizational plan for it that had caused her so many late nights during the past week.

"I tell you, Stell, he's the sexiest male you've ever seen."

Kacie's ears perked up at her neighbors' ongoing conversation.

"Not to me, he isn't. He's huge, for one thing, and his own mother couldn't call him handsome."

"Who needs handsome when you're six-foot-four?" the Weston devotee countered derisively. "That dark hair of his makes my fingers itch to touch it. And there's something absolutely romantic about those black eyes. He almost looks Latin."

"Good grief, Jean, who cares? We're not likely to meet him anyway." Stell rose, picking up her tray. "We'd better get back if we want to keep our jobs."

Her friend nodded, repeating her actions. Neither of them had noticed Kacie, who smiled wryly at Jean's reaction to the company owner. It was so reminiscent of her own response to Michael Blair when she was in college. What was it about successful older men that automatically made them attractive to young girls? Of course Michael had been handsome—a true Greek god.

She hadn't thought about him for nearly a year, she realized with a start. There had been a time when she was sure the pain of his defection just days before their wedding would remain with her forever.

Her own lunch finished, she deposited her tray on the long caddy before heading for the exit. It was odd how life worked out. Her work—and her dedication to it—had been one of the major causes of Michael's final betrayal. Yet, in the end, it had provided the escape route she'd needed. She had poured all her energies into it, using it as a shield from further involvement with anyone.

It was one characteristic she and the dark figure of Jake Weston obviously had in common. She smiled at the thought as she returned to her lab.

The summons from Bob Gaines came nearly at quitting time. In fact, Kacie had just finished clearing her desk for the day. How like him to leave it until the last moment. One more insignificant irritation in a long list of grievances. Just once she'd like to let her temper fly, she thought as she briskly pushed open the door leading to his office.

She took a seat, refusing to be intimidated by his deliberate failure to offer one. Short of an act of outright insubordination on Kacie's part, he didn't have the right to fire her, and they both knew it. She was good at her job, even if she was the new kid in the department, so he didn't dare carry his animosity too far.

"I read your report," he began without preamble.

"And?" she asked, voicing the word hanging between them.

"I suggest you leave the planning of operations like the Chicago one to *men* like Jake Weston." He placed the emphasis none too subtly on the gender. "Your figures look good enough on paper, but it's the actual practice that counts."

Kacie stared at him, shocked that she was hearing right. The thinly veiled malicious satisfaction in his eyes told her he meant every word. It took the last ounce of self-control she possessed to bite back her opinion of his intelligence.

"Is that your final verdict?" she questioned in a deceptively quiet voice.

He nooded slowly. "It is," he agreed in a militant tone.

So he thought she would make a scene, did he, Kacie observed. No way was she going to fling her slight company weight against his; he'd win hands down. No, all she had to do was wait. The error in Weston's calculations would show up sooner or later.

Sooner was swifter than even she expected. Two days passed, with several problems cropping up along the way. She had heard at lunch that Jake Weston was in the building, but thus far she hadn't seen him.

She had just returned from the cafeteria. She slipped into the long white coat she wore to protect her clothes and to ward off the chill of the climate-controlled room. The machines were as delicate as newborns, requiring a specific temperature and a relatively dust-free environment for maximum efficiency. She perched her blue-tinted glasses on the end of her nose and accepted the clipboard her partner, Ted, handed her.

"I've been over that calculation three times, and I still can't find the error," he explained, shrugging out of his own white jacket. "See what you can do, okay?"

She nodded, a frown of annoyance creasing her brow. She barely heard him leave as she stared at the sheets in her hand. All of this was so unnecessary. If only Gaines had listened!

She sat down in her chair, not bothering to recheck Ted's figures. Unless Bob gave his permission for them to revamp along the lines she had suggested, further calculations were useless anyway. While she was debating whether to appeal to the great man himself, she heard the lab door open.

"I don't believe that Ted Curtis, our senior man, is here at the moment, Jake."

Kacie heard Bob's voice oozing charm as she rose and turned. She found herself staring into the ebony eyes of the company wizard. In a flash her mind recorded the broad shoulders, the deep bronze skin, and the rugged face of the subject of her thoughts. He was tall, although that wasn't the first word that came to mind for a description. *Giant* was much more apt, she decided as she extended her hand when Bob introduced them.

"Miss Daniels," he greeted her with a brief inclination of his head. His grasp engulfed her fingers, and she sensed the control in his firm handshake. His voice matched his rough-hewn appearance, a deep growl that seemed to emanate from the broad, muscled chest. He was a man who appeared as if he'd be more at home in the north woods than in an office, Kacie mused.

If she was studying him, so, too, was he observing her, she realized with a sense of shock. She felt the assessing sweep of his eyes, and she thought about what he saw. She knew the cold temperature always washed away what little natural color her face had, and, without the softening effect of her thick hair, which was in its usual elastic tie at the nape of her neck, her distinctive cheekbones made her look all eyes and glasses. And considering the prim getup she wore, right down to the sensible shoes, and her no-nonsense manner, she wasn't surprised when his gaze dismissed her importance as a woman.

"I was telling Jake about our problems with the Chicago setup," Bob said, breaking the silence. "We came down to see how things were progressing."

Kacie eyed her immediate boss. "I'm afraid it isn't progressing at all," she announced bluntly. Her stare challenged him to ask why.

Predictably, he made no comment.

Jake Weston wasn't so silent. "Why not?" he snapped. "You have the procedure I mapped out, so what's the problem?"

Kacie glanced at him consideringly. Now was her chance. She turned, reaching for Ted's clipboard. Before she could open her mouth to explain, Bob saw his opportunity and used it.

"She has this crazy idea that your calculations are all wrong. I tried to tell her it wasn't *your* figures that were off, but *hers.*"

Black eyes searched her face. "You found an error in my calculations?"

She nodded.

"You showed it to Bob?"

"I did but—"

He didn't let her finish. "He told you to stick with the original plan?"

"Yes, he did—" she began, but again he cut her off.

"Look, lady, I know you've got a hotshot reputation, but stick with the stuff you know, and let me handle my job, okay?" He glared down at her, visibly irritated at her presuming to criticize his program.

Kacie had let him say his little piece; now it was her turn. She was damned tired of Gaines's undermining her ability, and she was annoyed that a man like Jake Weston would believe him without giving her a chance to defend herself.

Her temper did a slow burn. One wrong word—that's all she needed—and she would fry herself some male ears. This wasn't the only job around for which she was qualified.

She carefully turned the clipboard so that Jake could read the figures on the top sheet. "If I may explain, please, Mr. Weston," she ventured, her emphasis clearly on the last three words. Her eyes behind their round lenses were rock steady on his as she dared him to deny her the right. She saw his surprise before he slowly inclined his head.

"All right, let's have it." He glanced down at the paper she indicated.

"As you can see, these projected figures don't tally with the actual results from the computer." She flipped two sheets over, pointing to the third in a series of ten input steps. "Basically, the procedure is sound." She ignored his muttered comment. "The problem lies here. If you combine this intermediate action with the fifth progression, the error margin is reduced and the results on paper agree with the actual practice." She waited quietly as he took the board from her and silently studied the points she indicated. She couldn't resist glancing at Bob to see his reaction.

The thin, tight-lipped expression on his face told her he was not pleased by her actions. He knew as well as she did that he never should have ignored her proposal.

"This won't work a bit better." Jake's voice shattered the silence, refocusing Kacie's attention. "It may cut down the error margin, but it loses some of the flexibility

I intentionally built into the system. The whole idea behind this is to have all our offices work on one centralized program. To do that, it must be responsive to the different locales and their individual needs," he stated. "Your method destroys half the purpose."

"It does not," she denied hotly, all thoughts of control disappearing under this new attack. "And I can prove it!"

"There's no point in getting angry," he replied coolly. "I've looked over the changes you suggested, just as you asked, and I say they won't work for our uses. It's a good idea—inexperienced, but still good." He handed the papers back to her before extending a broad wrist to check the time. "I've got to be going if I'm to meet with the manager on schedule. We'll finish checking out the problems tomorrow morning."

Bob nodded, barely disguising his triumphant expression when Jake turned to him.

Kacie was so angry she was speechless. She watched the giant disappear through the doorway with Bob following on his heels like a faithful terrier. She glared at the data in her hand. Inexperienced! Damn him, he was right about that. If she were older and had more time with the company, she would have been in a better position to make him listen. But she was still on target with her approach. She knew it even if no one else did. She had been a fool to try to give a quickie explanation anyway. What she needed were her detailed findings. Her eyes lit up as she glanced at the clock on the wall. Ted would be back any minute now. If she hurried, she would have time to make it home, pick up her report, and get back before Weston left for the day. It would be a tight squeeze, but she could do it. She blanked her mind to the possibility that he might refuse to listen to her.

It just wasn't her day, she discovered when she finally reached her apartment. With the heavy traffic, it had taken nearly twice as long as usual just to get there, putting additional strain on her frayed nerves. She got out of the elevator at her floor, already fumbling for her door key. Naturally, it was at the bottom of her handbag.

"Damn," she swore with soft violence when the thing jammed in the lock. After a couple of yanks, she left it hanging, pulled the door open with a tug, and stalked inside, kicking off her sensible but confining shoes as she went. "No way am I wearing these clunky things for a second longer today," she mumbled, heading straight for the extra bedroom, which doubled as her workroom.

"Good!" She found her papers exactly where she had left them two days before. She lost a few precious moments hunting for her white sandals under her bed. By the time she had wrestled with her stubborn key and gotten back into the elevator, she felt decidedly ruffled. Her sleek, pulled-back hair had begun its escape from the two pins that secured the shorter wings on either side of her head. Shiny black wisps now feathered limply along her flushed cheeks to just below her ears. Her glasses had been discarded when she'd gotten into her car, but she only needed them for reading and close work, anyway.

The Peachtree Street parking lot for Weston Technology was empty when she finally got back.

"If he's gone after all this, I think I'll scream," she groaned aloud as she slid from the driver's seat. She hurried across the asphalt drive to the sidewalk. From there she had a view of the car slots reserved for management. The sleek, blunt-nosed Mercedes in the VIP space was the first good sign in a disastrous afternoon. Weston was still in the building.

Fortunately she knew where his office was, so she didn't waste time hunting through deserted corridors. She paused outside his door just long enough to get her breath before knocking smartly on the closed panel.

There was a moment's hesitation, then she heard a muffled, "Come in." The handle turned easily under her fingers and the door silently swung open. For a second she stood poised at the threshold. Her temper had carried her this far, but suddenly her computer brain was questioning her nerve.

"Can I help you?" he asked, courteously rising to his feet.

She stared at him in something akin to shock, realizing there was no recognition in his eyes. Surely he hadn't forgotten their earlier meeting! His deep voice mobilzed her. She stepped into the room, coming to a stop in front of him.

"I brought you the proof you asked for," she announced, slapping the stack of papers she held onto the dark oak desk top.

He stared first at the clipped sheaf, then back at her. There was puzzlement in his expression, which slowly changed to amazement as his gaze swept over her untidy hair, the blazing eyes, the slender form wrapped in a pale aqua knit dress, and the narrow white sandals below long, slender legs.

Kacie registered briefly that, without the lab coat and glasses, her altered appearance was the cause of his bemusement.

"Well, aren't you going to at least go over them?" she demanded impatiently when he didn't speak.

Visibly recovering from his confusion, he gestured to the chair at her side. "Why don't you sit down, Miss Daniels?" he offered quietly. "You look like you've been running up the stairs."

She shook her head. "No, thank you, I'll stand."

He shrugged, his eyes narrowing slightly at her upcompromising tone. "You don't mind if I do?" he asked rhetorically. Without bothering to wait for her answer, he sank into the massive padded chair and leaned back. He surveyed his visitor through half-closed lids, making no move to check the material she had flung onto his desk.

"I thought I had made myself clear this afternoon," he remarked in an even voice. Unspoken between them lay the fact that he was the boss and owner, she a mere employee. His power was absolute and should remain unquestioned.

"You might have, but I didn't. It was stupid of me to expect you to understand in a few minutes a situation that took me the better part of three nights to find myself." There was no conceit in her response, only a statement of truth.

There was a weighty pause during which Jake Weston's only reaction was a raised eyebrow.

"I know I'm inexperienced. You were right about that."

"I'm glad to know I was right about something," he murmured, his eyes never leaving her face.

Kacie took a deep breath, feeling the last remaining hold she had on her temper slipping. Any minute now she would say something really nasty.

She plunged in, more determined than ever to make this maddening giant take her seriously. "Will you just take these, please, and look them over tonight or tomorrow?" she asked, resorting to outright pleading. Somehow she instinctively knew better than to demand his compliance.

"No–o . . ." he said slowly, something altering in his expression. "I'll—" He got no further.

Kacie had had it. "Damn you and Bob Gaines," she hissed. "The great big male superstars!" Her comment was unforgivable, and she knew it the moment the words left her mouth. She saw anger akin to her own darken his face, but her sharp tongue was not to be silenced. "I quit. I've spent three months putting up with the fragile masculine ego, but not any more." She swung around, her whole being intent on escape. She would go to California, she thought wildly. She was fed up with Atlanta, anyway. She almost made it to the door when she was jerked to a stop by a strong grasp on her shoulder. She yelped as his hand got tangled in the long switch of hair hanging down her back, and at the same moment she felt the elastic holding her hair in place break.

"See what you've done," she snapped, whirling to face him. Her eyes blurred with tears of frustration and pain from her stinging scalp.

She glared at her attacker, then down to the hand that still held her prisoner. He was so close she could feel the heat of his massive body through the thin fabric of her dress. She watched, mesmerized, as his fingers slowly opened one by one, releasing the shiny cascade over her shoulders.

"Did I hurt you?" he asked, a note of concern in his voice.

She shook her head silently, her anger spent as suddenly as it had begun. She kept her eyes lowered. She was appalled at her outburst, called for or not. She felt his hand on her shoulders, heard with stunned surprise his low chuckle of amusement. She raised her gaze, focusing on his rugged face. He was laughing!

"I'll say one thing for you, Irish. You've got one hell of a temper," he teased.

She blinked in confusion. How did he know her nationality?

"I checked your personnel profile," he supplied, seeing the question in her expression. He pushed her gently back toward his desk. "Now, you are going to sit down and keep that cute little mouth of yours shut while I finish the sentence you so rudely interrupted." The voice matched his touch, but there was a stern gleam in his eyes that warned her to do exactly what he said.

Kacie allowed him to seat her, still puzzling over his revelation. Why had he checked her folder? It didn't make sense. She glanced across the desk, catching his shrewd eyes on her. They stared at each other in assessing silence.

"Now, as I started to say, I'll go over your proposal *now*. I had intended to go into it with you tomorrow." He smiled slightly at the amazement on her face. He waited for her to say something.

She wasn't capable of uttering a word. After what she had said, how she had acted, she had expected anything but this.

"Can you stay?"

She nodded, her hair swinging around her shoulders to caress her breasts. She was suddenly conscious of how she must look. She raised her hands, intending to pull the dark cloud away from her face, and saw him frown.

"Leave it," he ordered.

She hesitated, self-conscious about obeying. She never

wore her hair down except at home. Keeping it long and lustrous was her one concession to vanity, but leaving it free was totally impractical for the type of work she did.

She slowly dropped her arms, realizing she might be risking his anger by refusing his command.

Jake inclined his head before turning to study the report before him. The minutes ticked away, marked by an occasional whisper of paper when he moved from one page to the next.

While he read, Kacie had an opportunity to recover her natural composure, and she took the time to glance around her.

A person could tell a lot about a man from his office. She knew from the company grapevine that Jake Weston had a duplicate of this suite in his New York branch, and presumably one was to be added in Chicago. When Kacie had first heard the story, her immediate reaction had been derisive of the incredible conceit. Later she had learned from a trade journal interview that there was a much more practical reason for the arrangement. Since he liked to keep in close touch with all his operations, he felt it was more convenient to be able to come into a different branch and be completely at home. It saved time. She had been amazed that, in that same article, he had admitted to decorating his suites himself.

Kacie was intrigued by the subtle colors he favored. One wall was a deep shade of sable brown, a perfect backdrop for the pale-oatmeal overstuffed couch and grouping of matching chairs. The carpet was a celery shade, which tied together the wide expanse of sun-tinted glass windows and the remaining light-beige walls. But it was his choice of paintings that really captured her interest.

Rural scenes, every one. Not a building or a person in sight. The canvases were vivid, full of greens, golds, and earth tones. For a city dweller, he appeared to love the country. His room reflected it, down to the healthy indoor plants dotting the area.

"If you're finished inspecting my taste..." Weston said unexpectedly, managing to glance up and catch her in her perusal.

Kacie refused to apologize for her study. After all, what else was there for her to do? She gathered her self-confidence about her like a cloak. She must restore this meeting to some sort of professional footing, on her part at least. He, thus far, had managed to retain his temper, even in the face of great provocation.

"You have an unusual office," she smiled coolly, her habitual poise reasserting itself.

He nodded, a knowing gleam in his eye. He ignored her comment and gestured to her report. "And you have quite a comprehensive study here."

She lifted her chin slightly at the vague note of surprise she thought she detected, but she said nothing. No way was she going to interrupt one of his sentences again.

Jake's lips twitched at her obvious restraint. Evidently he hadn't missed the defiant tilt of her jaw. "Not only have you found the problem, but you've simplified the system in the process," he continued, definite admiration replacing his earlier expression.

Kacie was somewhat appeased by his attitude. It wasn't his praise so much as the fact that he had listened. "Thank you," she said simply.

Jake grinned openly. "No, 'I told you so'?" he asked.

"No," she responded, finding her sense of humor nudged by his question. Something about his amusement was contagious. The devil lurking in his midnight eyes seemed to dare her to join in.

"A pity," he drawled on a disappointed note.

Kacie couldn't help it: she started to laugh. "Why?" she had to ask.

"I'm not going to tell you," he declared, shaking his head. For a moment their gazes locked. Kacie knew her defenses were down. She suspected he did, too. Had he changed the level of their conversation on purpose? But why? What possible reason could he have?

Her eyes suddenly widened with curiosity and wariness. There had been no one in her life since Michael, and she liked it that way. She recognized and resented this distinct stirring of personal interest.

"Irish, I—" Jake began, only to be interrupted by the telephone. He held her stare for a second longer before picking up the receiver.

Kacie felt the pull of his personality even as he gave his attention to the caller. As much as possible she mentally blocked her ears to the conversation until she caught a change in his voice.

"Where are you now, Abbey?...Of course I don't mind; there are two bedrooms...I just wish I'd known you were coming..." He paused and glanced at his watch. "I should be finishing up shortly, then we'll go out to dinner."

He hung up the phone and sat staring at it for a moment, an unreadable expression on his face. When he glanced back at her, the challenging light was gone from his eyes.

"I'll see you in the lab in the morning," he directed, reverting to the impersonality of a boss.

Kacie rose with a brief inclination of her head, realizing the cause. For a space of time there had been a spark of awareness between them. The call had changed all that. Abbey, whoever she was, obviously had a claim on him. Right now, she wasn't sure whether she was glad or sorry. She knew which she should be.

2

KACIE MEASURED AN extra scoop of coffee into the basket of the percolator. This morning she needed all the help she could get, she thought with a grimace. Her mirror told her she looked like the lone survivor of a lost war, and her bed resembled a battleground. What sleep she had finally managed to get had been haunted by specters of the past. She had relived every painful moment of Michael's betrayal. She damned Jake Weston for stirring the coals of her slumbering emotions. She didn't want to remember. She didn't want to feel again.

There had been a time when Michael was her whole world. Except for her two extraordinarily gifted parents, Michael had been the only person to scale the wall of reserve Kacie had built to keep others at bay. An only child with an unbelievably high IQ, she had been quiet to the point of shyness. Being intellectually superior had made her the brunt of her peers' often cruel humor. With the death of her parents in a car crash the week of her college graduation, she was alone. Then, when she started working for her master's, she had met Michael Blair.

As a guest lecturer in one of her programming classes, he had made an immediate hit with the students, not only because of his expertise, but also his movie-star good looks. Kacie had felt drawn to him from the moment she'd sat in his group. Later, bumping into him in the hallway, she had found he was equally interested in her. A quick cup of coffee in the college snack bar had been the beginning of a lightning-fast courtship—eight weeks—which had culminated in his proposal.

Luckily some remnant of her sanity had prevailed, because she'd pleaded with him to wait until she got her degree before they married. At the time, she hadn't realized how much he resented her intense involvement in her field, particularly since that was why they had met. At first, their relationship had remained close, but bit by bit he'd begun arriving at her apartment later each night, then canceling altogether. When one well-meaning friend had told her about Debbie, she hadn't believed her. She loved Michael, so it followed that she trusted him.

She'd found out how little he deserved her loyalty three days before their wedding day. Even now she could recall every detail of that hot, muggy July afternoon— the sight of the petite blonde wrapped in the velour robe Kacie herself had given Michael for his thirty-first birthday. She hadn't needed to see him coming out of the bedroom they had planned together, still adjusting his trousers, to clarify what had happened.

She took down a mug from the counter and filled it. The black liquid burned her tongue as she sipped, but

she hardly noticed the pain. The floodgates damming her
emotions were open at last. The agony she had felt at
Michael's cruel denunciation washed over her, his words
once again ringing in her ears.

"You're a human computer, Kacie. No heart, just tiny
little component parts. I've waited almost two years to
marry you. Why? Because you wanted your degree. You
wouldn't even live with me. Oh, you'd share my bed,
all right, but half the time I could have gotten more
satisfaction out of one of those machines in the lab."

Kacie took another swallow, longing to erase forever
what had come next.

"I found a *real* woman, someone smart enough to
know how to let me be the man, her man. For all your
brains, Kacie, you aren't capable of any deep feelings.
Not love, not hate, not anything. Look at you now.
You're not even angry. Just once I wish you could show
some honest emotion. Cry a little. You might find out
you're human."

Kacie stared into her empty mug, not even remembering drinking it dry. She never had wept. Not then,
not later when the nights had been years long. She had
locked it all away, pouring her efforts and her energies
into building a career. There she was safe, self-confident.
As the months had passed, the pent-up emotions hardened into a stronger wall, protecting her from any involvement. She became what Michael had labeled her.

Until yesterday. Jake Weston had somehow signaled
the end of her self-imposed isolation. He had made her
lose her temper, almost reduced her to tears, and given
her laughter all in the space of an afternoon. And it was
agony.

This coming alive was torture. Tiny stiletto shafts of

pain pierced her heart, her mind, and destroyed her sleep, denying her any relief. She bitterly resented the attraction she felt to the dark giant. She hated his ability to stir her dormant emotions. Now, this morning, she had to face him, work with him. She buried her head in her hands at the thought. She desperately needed time. There wasn't any. Slowly she raised her eyes, staring straight into the bold-faced kitchen clock. The decision was hers. She could run—call in and say she was ill—or she could get dressed, pick up her handbag and her courage, and go to work.

After fortifying herself for the big confrontation, Kacie was disconcerted to find that Jake wasn't even in the building when she arrived at work. She was alone in the lab, after Ted had gone for lunch, when he finally appeared. The first inkling she had that he was even in the room with her was his deep, growling greeting. She looked up, peering over her glasses to stare at the massive body blocking the doorway.

"Mr. Weston," she murmured faintly, the composure she had finally achieved late in the morning cracking slightly at the sight of him.

"I'm late, I know," he apologized, coming farther into the lab and shutting the door behind him. "I got held up in a meeting."

Momentarily Kacie wondered if it was with Abbey of the phone call, then she determinedly banished the idea. She promised herself she would stick to business. There, at least, she was on safe ground.

"That's all right," she responded in a conventionally polite tone.

"The perfect response, Miss Daniels." He came over to stand beside her.

Kacie was struck by the distinct note of irritation, bordering almost on anger, in his voice. She waited for his next comment.

"Shall we get down to work?" he asked when she didn't speak. "I want to start with step one."

Obviously he had no intention of explaining the source of his mood, Kacie observed. She nodded, shifting her chair so he could pull a seat in next to hers. It took a great deal of self-control not to put feet instead of inches between them. With her forefinger she nervously pushed her glasses farther up on the bridge of her nose.

"I see you've already begun."

"Just now," she affirmed, breathing a faint sigh of relief. Some of the tension she'd felt when he'd entered slowly eased. Apparently he was as determined as she to forget yesterday. Probably, from his point of view, there was nothing worth remembering. She wondered briefly why the vagrant thought gave her no pleasure.

"I thought a bit more about your report, and, using it as a basis, we may be able to trim off some more excess. How does this sound . . . ?"

And so it began. Kacie found that Jake was more than a match for her. The initial programming plan had been a complicated piece of work. Her revisions had simplified it on one level, but he had taken it yet a step further. She was amazed at the brilliance of his mind, the grasp he had on her concept. The afternoon flew by. She was conscious of a deep sense of satisfaction in the free-flowing give and take of ideas.

After their awkward beginning, she had expected some difficulties. But there were none. It was as though, by mutual consent, they met on neutral ground, two professionals with a common goal. Kacie felt no need to hide behind her barriers, and little by little the real woman she was emerged. She became engrossed in their computations, temporarily losing her unsettling awareness of Jake as a man.

"That's it," he announced in a deep sigh. He leaned back in his chair, stretching tiredly.

Kacie studied the final streamlined system with a definite sense of accomplishment. She glanced sideways at Jake's sprawled figure. Unwillingly, her eyes wandered over the taut muscles of his chest before settling on his face. "That last idea of yours was a stroke of pure genius," she offered sincerely.

"You didn't do so badly yourself, Irish," he replied lazily. He turned his head slightly to check the wall clock. "Looks like I owe you three hours overtime. How about if I give you a bonus by taking you out to eat?"

Kacie stiffened at his use of the nickname. All afternoon she had been Miss Daniels. With a few words he had altered everything. She stared at him warily as he gazed back at her. "That won't be necessary," she refused in a rapidly cooling tone. "I can easily fix something at home."

"You could, but you're not going to." He rose, towering over her. "Consider it an order from the boss."

Kacie read the determination in his stance. She stared at him, resentment invading every muscle of her body. She wished desperately she was standing, until she realized she would be even closer to him than she was now. She hated the trapped feeling he inspired in her. For a long moment she silently continued to defy him.

"All right," she finally agreed, her voice echoing her defeat.

He nodded approvingly. "I've got to make one call first. It won't take a minute."

"If you like, you can use this phone while I freshen up," she offered, gladly taking the hint that he wanted to be alone.

Jake was waiting for her when she returned to the lab. His glance passed over her makeup-free face, the sleek cap of pulled back hair, and the beige shirtwaist dress that did absolutely nothing for her.

Kacie endured his scrutiny with outward composure, keeping her face completely devoid of any expression. This morning she had purposefully chosen the least attractive garment she owned. A defense, she acknowledged to herself, against the emotions this man stirred in her. Since she never wore cosmetics at work, mainly because it was a bother to worry about fading lipstick and a shiny nose, she didn't carry any with her to relieve her colorless appearance. She sensed Jake's disapproval and was satisfied with her image. The moments away from him had allowed her to pull her cloak of remoteness about her. Within its folds she felt secure, safe from any unwanted advances. If she had to share a meal with him, she definitely wanted to remain Miss Daniels, not the volatile Irish he had dubbed her.

"I wonder why you wear that nun outfit, Kacie Daniels," Jake mused aloud, openly enjoying her resulting gasp of outrage at his comment. "Are you afraid that if you let your hair down, I might see the real you?"

For a moment a blaze of pure indignation brought a flush to her ivory cheeks. Kacie saw the triumph in his expression a split second before she opened her lips and destroyed her own protective aloofness. It took every ounce of willpower she possessed to clamp her tongue between her teeth and count to ten.

"I admire your self-control," he taunted with a grin, obviously well aware of the struggle going on within her.

"I wonder who'll win—Miss Daniels or Irish?" He paused as though waiting for an answer.

Kacie wasn't capable of uttering a word. One would be too many. She glanced briefly past his broad shoulders to the door. The need to escape was overwhelming. Lord, she must have been mad to agree to dine with him.

Almost as if he was aware of her fervent desire, Jake grasped her arm. His grip was light but Kacie didn't doubt its restraining power if she made a move to flee.

"Come on, Kacie Daniels, you're safe for the moment."

"I'm safe, period," she enunciated clearly, finding her voice at last.

He smiled, lines of laughter crinkling the corners of velvet-rich eyes. "Sure you are, Irish. Didn't I just say so?"

She glared at him, the impulse to stamp her foot surprisingly strong. Damn his Yankee hide! Didn't he listen to anyone but himself? Irritated, she barely noticed their quick passage through the deserted corridors to an equally empty parking lot.

It was only when she heard the final thud of the Mercedes' door that she realized she was committed—for the next few hours, anyway. After that, he didn't stand a snowball's chance in Hades of forcing her into going out with him alone again.

The restaurant he chose was small but elegant, exuding the discreet atmosphere of expensive dining. The intimate, candlelit tables grouped about a glass-smooth dance floor were filled with obviously wealthy patrons, and Kacie momentarily felt out of place in her simple dress. As they were escorted to their table in a small alcove overlooking the establishment's flowering gardens, she noticed the female glances stealing toward her companion. It was impossible to deny his attraction. The navy-blue business suit he wore stretched over powerful muscles, highlighting the raw masculinity of its wearer. Reluctantly Kacie acknowledged his magnetism. Despite her outward composure, she knew her mask was a fragile thing.

Under Jake's charm she found it impossible to retain even a modicum of her coolness. He started his assault with questions about her job, which demanded answers. By the time she realized his tactics, their dinners had arrived. From then on the evening progressed along the path he chose.

Kacie found he was well informed on a variety of topics. While his opinions were very definite, they were by no means the only ones he acknowledged. She slowly relaxed. Lulled by the smooth white wine and the delicious food, her fears dissipated. She raised her glass to her lips, lifting her lashes to stare across the cleared table, directly into Jake's eyes.

"I can see why you're so successful," she commented wryly, thinking how effectively dark eyes hid revealing thoughts and expressions.

She didn't need to cross her *t*'s. Jake caught her meaning immediately.

He raised his brandy in salute. "I couldn't let you spoil your dinner."

An arched brow framed her unspoken question.

"Being uptight is bad for the digestion," he explained obligingly. "Besides, I like to see you laugh." He twisted his snifter in his hands, his gaze never leaving her face. "Would you retreat again if I said something?"

Kacie tensed, warning bells sounding in her mind.

Although surprisingly relaxed, she still retained her instincts for self-protection. She wasn't sure if she needed them, but she had no intention of lowering her defenses any more than she already had.

He shook his head. "See what I mean? You're all set to jump without knowing whether you need to. Don't you ever just take life as it comes?"

"Do you?" she countered. "From what I've seen so far, I doubt it."

"We're not talking about me, Irish, remember?"

"Don't call me that!"

"Why? Does it remind you of what's under that cool outer shell?" he asked, his eyes gently mocking.

"That's not very kind," she observed, surprisingly less angered by his words now than she would have been earlier in the evening. "And that's the second time since we arrived that you've brought it up. Do you have a particular reason for needling me, or are you just being your usual self?" The need to strike back in even a limited way was undeniable. He wasn't the only one who could ask outrageous questions.

"I'm not a kind person, you know. I can't think where you could get the idea that I was."

Kacie glimpsed something both lazy and dangerous in his ebony eyes, yet she felt no fear. There was a strange exhilaration in their verbal fencing. Normally she never would have been brave enough nor blunt enough to carry on this type of conversation, but some devil of mischief demanded that she stand and fight back.

"Is that a warning?"

For a moment he was silent, looking at her thoughtfully. "I suppose it is. I may play to win, but I believe in being fair."

Kacie felt a faint stirring of fear. This was no longer a game. This man was brilliant, well accustomed to success where others had failed. Had she unknowingly provoked the very thing she wished to avoid? Did he see her as a challenge? The thought made her heart pause in its rhythm. She stared at him, wide-eyed with anxiety. All she wanted was to be left in peace, yet he sat there like a giant predator calmly announcing his intentions. Her tongue flickered nervously over suddenly dry lips, drawing his eyes to her mouth. A dark gleam replaced the clouds masking his thoughts.

Kacie was held motionless by unseen bonds. His gaze was a visual caress.

"Don't look so trapped, Irish," he murmured in a husky rumble. "Trust in yourself more. You can, you know."

Kacie heard his whispered words in disbelief. What did he mean? Confusion replaced some of her fear. She felt his fingers encircle her hand as it tensely gripped her glass. She watched, mesmerized, as he slowly eased her fingers away from her snifter. His grasp was warm and somehow comforting as her slender hand lay enfolded in his large one. He carried her fingers to his lips, his eyes never leaving her face. His breath was warm against her skin. The kiss he placed in the center of her sensitized palm was as light as thistledown, yet it seemed to brand her as his possession.

Reflexes and her clamoring senses made her try to tug free. She failed. The lean fingers tightened on her fine-boned wrist, holding her prisoner.

"Come on, I'll take you home," he commanded softly, rising to his feet and pulling her with him.

"But my car," she protested in a daze.

"Leave it. I'll pick you up in the morning, on my way in."

She opened her mouth to object, but he stopped her with a quick shake of her imprisoned hand. "Don't fight me, Kacie. With one thing and another, it's been a tough day."

She stared at him, wanting to refuse but knowing she would waste her time by trying. There was no mistaking the implacable expression. She nodded mutely, unable to bring herself to thank him for his consideration, since a good portion of *her* tough day, as he'd called it, was his fault.

She was tired, she admitted as she sank into the plush leather interior of his car. The contoured bucket seat supported and soothed her weary body while Jake expertly negotiated the heavy mid-evening traffic. She gazed out the window at the glowing city lights, grateful for his silence.

She was on an emotional merry-go-round. Her senses were alive as never before. She was vividly aware of Jake, the scent of his woodsy cologne, the feel of his body warmth in the close confines of the front seat. Even Atlanta took on whole new dimensions of color and sound. She was engulfed with unfamiliar sensations, her mind and body reeling from their impact. Her home beckoned as a haven in a world gone crazy because of one man. She was frightened by what was happening to her, but at the moment she was helpless to fight it. She sighed deeply.

"Almost there, Irish," Jake's voice reached out to stroke her, the velvet rumble curiously calming. "It's a good thing I lifted your address from the personnel files— you've been singularly lax about providing directions," he teased softly.

She turned her head to study his rugged profile. "I knew you would have asked if you didn't already know where I lived," she murmured astutely, too tired to worry about a tactful reply.

He glanced at her, seemingly sensing her scrutiny, and smiled slightly. "You look all eyes," he observed, ignoring her comment. He eased his car into the visitor's slot at her apartment house. After switching off the engine, he slid out from his side, admitting a cool waft of evening air as he opened his door.

Kacie waited, hardly aware she was doing so, until she felt the same soft breeze drift across her face. She glanced up to find him towering over her, a darkened shadow in the dimly lit parking area.

"Have you gone to sleep on me?" he asked, gentle humor evident in his tone.

"No," she denied, hastily coming to life. Apparently he took pity on her exhaustion, merely securing her arm in a possessive grip to escort her to her door.

It was nearly eleven o'clock by the time Kacie finally tumbled into bed. As she lay awake waiting for sleep to calm the tumult of her senses, she relived the effects of Jake's measured behavior. All evening he had succeeded in throwing her completely off stride. Each time she was able to reconstruct her defenses, he tore them down like so many matchsticks. Yet when she was most vulnerable, he had not taken advantage of her.

There was nothing like expecting to fight a man off at the door and then receiving only a brief, gentle kiss on the forehead to completely demolish whatever was left of a woman's shattered poise. It must have been the surprise of his mild good night that had made her accept his driving her to work without even a token protest.

The next morning Kacie stood in front of her closet,

irritation rippling through her. Behind her on the bed lay discarded three dresses, mute testimony to her uncharacteristic indecision.

"Blast, blast, *blast!*" she swore vehemently, snatching out a blue-gray wraparound. "I will not dress up for you, Jake Weston."

She hurriedly stepped into the lightweight jersey, her eyes on the clock, which was rapidly ticking away precious minutes. She was hot, ruffled, and aggravated, and she hadn't even faced Jake yet. She ignored the oval mirror above her vanity. The last thing she wanted to see was her face. She knew the gray dress washed her pale skin to white, almost as much as the beige shirtwaist did. That fact, coupled with hair drawn back even tighter than usual and eyes bearing the distinct signs of two fitful nights in a row, made her look her worst—or so she hoped. She knew darned well she felt it.

She was still intent on presenting a cool, businesslike front, when she heard Jake's brisk knock. She opened the door, bag in hand, ready to leave and determined not to invite him in. She focused her greeting on a point just to the right of his left ear.

"Prompt, I see," he murmured, his lips twitching slightly. He stood aside while she stepped out and locked her door.

"I didn't want to keep you waiting," she replied politely.

"You won't."

She looked at him sharply, struck by something in his tone and the odd phrasing, but he was already heading for the elevator. She had no choice but to follow.

The ride to the ground floor was completed in almost total silence. The charming host of the previous evening was absent, Kacie noticed immediately. Jake appeared immersed in some deep problem and unaware of her careful scrutiny.

Today he wore a charcoal-gray suit with a pale tailored shirt. Conservative and quiet on most men, it dramatically enhanced Jake's black hair and added a touch of polished sophistication to his raw masculinity. Unwilling attraction stirred to life. Mentally berating herself for giving in to the very feelings she had vowed to fight, Kacie concentrated on keeping her calm, unaffected mask intact.

They were nearly at the office before he seemed to remember her presence. He glanced at her as they stopped for a red light. "Sorry about ignoring you," he apologized.

"That's okay." She paused before probing delicately, "Business?"

His lips twisted in a small grimace. "Yes and no.

Kacie was intrigued, her curiosity aroused. She waited for him to elaborate.

He eased the car forward as the signal turned green. "I need to ask one of my people here to fly to Chicago and then to New York with me."

Her brows quirked in astonishment. Was that all? "So?" she asked, her tone clearly indicating she didn't see the problem.

"This person probably won't want to go. But there isn't anyone else with the expertise and firsthand knowledge I need."

Although his eyes remained on the street ahead, Kacie sensed his interest in her answer.

"Have you asked?"

He shook his head, glancing at her.

"Hadn't you better, before you start worrying about what to do next?" Suddenly a feeling of dismay washed over her. She stared at him, comprehension dawning. "Me?" she asked ungrammatically. The last thing she wanted was to spend any more time in Jake's unnerving presence. She swallowed, her throat tight with apprehension. She didn't need his nod of assent as confirmation.

In the seconds before she spoke again, all sorts of ideas raced through her mind—including flatly refusing and turning in her resignation. Only long practiced discipline kept the chaos locked away behind a placid veneer. Two factors stood out above all others. One: Weston Technologies was a top firm in her field, and she had a super chance to go as far as she liked. With her work on this program, even Bob Gaines's dislike was no detriment. Two: unfortunately, that didn't make up for Jake's disturbing effect on her.

"I could train someone else," she offered, grasping at any possibility, no matter how remote.

"No." His response was uncompromising.

"You could do it yourself." She tried one final time. She knew she had no real choice if she wanted to retain her position. In fact, if it were anyone else making the offer, she'd jump at the chance for the experience. But Jake? Could she continue to subdue the needs he triggered in her and still do her job well?

"You know you want to do it. Why don't you give in?" Jake suggested with a grin that said he knew where the problem lay. "Unless you have someone who would object to your temporary absence..."

Without thought, she shook her head. "I don't have any ties." Maybe she could handle her feelings for Jake if it were only a short trip. "How long?" she asked, hoping his answer would give her the reassurance she needed.

He shrugged. "As long as it takes," he responded unhelpfully.

She turned to stare out the window as he pulled to a stop in the VIP space, and a fatalistic calm settled over her at the combined threat and promise contained in Jake's words. She had no choice now; she had to go forward, knowing in advance that nothing was settled between them. "When do we leave?"

She didn't look at him when she heard the whisper of leather as he shifted in his seat. She jumped when his hand passed before her line of vision to grasp her chin. His hold was a firm demand for her to face him. Reluctantly, she met his ebony stare.

"Whoever did a number on you, Irish, ought to be shot at dawn," he remarked in a gentle voice that didn't hide his savage indictment of the culprit. "Try trusting yourself a little. I know you don't believe in me—I'd be willing to bet not in any man." His thumb moved caressingly along the smooth line of her jaw. "Nothing's going to happen to you unless you let it."

She shook her head in confusion. One minute Jake spoke of business, the next he became intimately perceptive, saying things no one else had ever suspected or dared to intimate. Was this some new technique to gain her capitulation, or was he just amusing himself at her expense?

He smiled, seeming to sense her chaotic feelings. "Don't worry so much. I promise you this trip is necessary. It's no trick."

"I didn't think it was," she replied, slightly relieved

at the reason he apparently believed to be the cause of her dilemma. Maybe she hadn't betrayed herself as much as she thought. She saw the satisfied gleam in his eyes at her answer.

"That's a start, anyway," he murmured, releasing her to get out of the car.

Kacie wasn't sure whether he had intended her to hear his comment or not. Somehow she suspected he hadn't. The implication behind those few softly spoken words wasn't something she wanted to contemplate. She opened her door and slid out before he had a chance to reach her.

"You still haven't told me when we leave," she reminded him, falling into step at his side. She was vividly conscious of his size as she tried to keep pace with his long-legged stride. She had to tilt her head at an uncomfortable angle just to meet his eyes.

He glanced sideways, immediately slowing his walk. "You're going?"

She nodded.

"Can you be ready by Monday morning? That will give you the weekend to pack."

"I think so," she agreed, startled at the rush. "How long—"

"You'll need clothes for ten to fourteen days, at least," he explained, overriding her next question. He pushed open the main door, allowing her to precede him. "Be sure to include a couple of evening gowns as well." He punched the elevator button. "I'll pick you up at nine-thirty to go to the airport."

"You've made reservations already? Were you that sure I'd agree?" she demanded, stepping into the empty elevator.

Jake grinned, showing even white teeth. "I was sure you'd agree eventually. You're too intelligent to let anything put you off such a golden opportunity. But you're wrong about booking our seats. There's no need. My Lear will get us there."

Kacie's eyes widened at his calm pronouncement. His own jet. How could she have forgotten reading about his Lear, she wondered, momentarily diverted by her memory lapse.

A flicker of concern lit the ebony eyes. "You do fly, don't you?"

She nodded. "Yes, of course."

"Is there a problem? You can be ready, can't you?"

She briefly debated saying no just to see how he would overrule her this time. Luckily, sanity prevailed, and she contented herself with a quick yes. The elevator slid open at that moment, stopping at her floor.

Jake pushed the hold button. "I'll pick you up for lunch. It's time you met the branch boss," he directed.

Kacie inclined her head, her expression calm. It was much easier to retain her poise in the well-ordered world of her office. "Shall I begin implementing the system?"

"Definitely. Get as much help as you need—borrow if necessary," he ordered.

The doors slid closed before she could ask whether Bob had been informed about the go-ahead to reprogram or not. What was she supposed to do now? Carry on, assuming her boss had been told, or let him know herself in case he hadn't? Mindful of the conflict between them, she decided on the latter course.

Minutes later she faced Bob across the width of his desk, wondering why she'd been such a fool.

"So the whiz kid has done it again," he observed

sarcastically. He stared at her with unconcealed dislike.

Kacie ignored his cutting comment, retaining her composure with more effort than usual. She felt her temper rising, and she blamed Jake for its sudden vehemence. Mentally she admitted it was at times like this when she wished she'd stayed at Comco with her much more enlightened boss, ignoring the whopping pay inducement and the opportunities at Weston. But never had she been so close to telling Bob so. Damn Jake for his influence over her.

When she didn't rise to his bait, Bob's eyes lost some of their glitter. "Do you need any help?" he asked in a more reasonable tone.

"Ted and I should be able to handle it," she responded calmly.

He nodded. "Okay." He paused thoughtfully. "At least we'll have a chance to complete our reprogramming before Jake flies the other branch's personnel in for training."

Sheer surprise held Kacie motionless. So Jake hadn't told Bob about the proposed visit to Chicago and New York. "Probably," she agreed quickly, deciding it wasn't her place to inform him. "I'd better get to work." She turned for the door.

"You did a nice job." Bob's voice held a wealth of reluctance in spite of his compliment.

Kacie swung around, disbelief dispelling some of her coolness. She expected to see mockery in the older man's face; instead, all she saw was the top of his head as he seemingly gave his full attention to the correspondence on his desk. She found she was staring at him. Had he actually said something good about her work albeit unwillingly? When he didn't look up—although he had to be aware she was still in the room—she was forced to believe it. A tiny smile curved her lips. A crack in the wall of dislike, at last. Wisely she quietly let herself out of the room.

After the previous weeks of plaguing starts and stops, Kacie was delighted when the new streamlined program was finally implemented. While as a systems analyst her function was mainly to oversee, at this point she couldn't suppress the intense feeling of satisfaction she derived from watching Ted punch in the new procedure. She found she held her breath as each step was programmed, then accepted. Lunchtime arrived before she knew it, and with it the realization that so far there hadn't been one hang-up.

Kacie slipped out of her lab coat, eager to tell Jake the good news. At that moment personal feelings were miles away in the face of her professional pride and accomplishment.

"I might be late getting back," she explained to Ted, a smile lighting her usually grave features. She pulled her handbag from her bottom desk drawer, which she then shut with a well-placed foot.

The resulting bang brought Ted's head up. He glanced at her in surprise, apparently at both her words and the accompanying grin. He shrugged. "Okay, you never take your full time anyway."

Kacie had her hand on the door when his words reached her ears. With her back to him she hesitated for a fraction of a second before continuing into the hall with a murmured good-bye. Once she was outside, some of her elation faded as self-awareness struck. She hadn't missed Ted's amazement at her ordinary comment. Suddenly she saw herself as others did—the robot, the woman with only work on her mind. She frowned, irked at the image she had projected since her school days. Except for the brief period of Michael's influence she had always been seriously committed, she assured herself, seeking to subdue the intrusive thought.

"Problems?" a deep, rich voice rumbled from behind her.

Kacie swung around, hastily smoothing her expression. "Not at all," she denied coolly. "As a matter of fact, just the opposite." She eyed Jake's solid figure far more composedly than she thought herself capable of doing.

"I hope I didn't keep you waiting, Jake."

Kacie turned at the sound of another male voice booming from the opposite direction. She found herself staring into twinkling blue eyes several shades lighter than her own.

"Bill, I'd like you to meet Kacie Daniels. Kacie, Bill Murphy," Jake introduced in a businesslike tone.

"Mr. Murphy." Kacie extended her hand in greeting.

"Bill," he replied with a grin.

Jake glanced at the man inches shorter than he. "Finished?"

He nodded. "For the moment, anyway."

Kacie was impelled forward by Jake's large hand at the middle of her back. She was sandwiched between the two men in the crowded elevator. Jake's broad frame shielded her from jostling even while it intimidated her by its sheer size.

When the door opened she stepped out, automatically heading for the cafeteria. A steel grip on her arm stopped her before she had taken two strides.

"Not that way," Jake commanded, turning her toward the main entrance.

Since he hadn't released her arm, Kacie had no choice but to walk in the direction he indicated.

"I see Jake was being his usual uninformative self," Bill remarked, pushing the plate-glass door wide. "He didn't tell you we were eating out."

Kacie exited first, with Jake only a step behind. "Obviously not," she murmured.

"What she means is, I didn't have time to this morning. We were too busy discussing other things," Jake drawled significantly.

Kacie glared at him on seeing the amazed lift of Bill's eyebrows. "Now tell him why," she demanded, hating the knowing amusement in his ebony gaze. Damn his hide, she swore silently, shooting daggers with her eyes. She was hardly aware of taking the passenger's place in the front seat of his Mercedes. How dare he put her in such a position, she thought in rising indignation. She knew damned well he and Bill had spent the morning in conference, so there was no way she could pretend they had met during ordinary business hours.

By the time he took his place beside her and started the car without explaining, she was ready to strangle him, bare-handed if necessary. Her searing stare should have scorched his skin, but he seemed impervious to it. He was grinning, a crooked smile slashing across his rough features, revealing his gleaming white teeth. He glanced over his shoulder to the silent man in the back seat, a witness to Kacie's discomfort and growing embarrassment.

"She doesn't look like she has a temper, does she?" he questioned in a man-to-man voice.

Kacie stared straight ahead, her hands tightly clenched in an effort at control. At that moment she disliked Jake intensely. Why was he so bent on getting to her, she wondered in despair. What had she done to deserve the way he was treating her? She turned her head to survey him as he alternately concentrated on his driving and on talking to Bill. For the moment, he seemed to have forgotten her. Kacie's eyes were bleak as she realized the type of gossip his remarks could start. As her name dropped from his lips, she forced herself to pay attention to what he was saying.

"Kacie was kind enough to agree to accompany me to Chicago and New York to set up our program," he explained. He chuckled. "Darned nice of her, too, after I practically kidnapped her into having supper with me last night and then wouldn't bring her back to pick up her car." He flicked her a teasing look, and she felt some of the stiffness leave her body. "I felt like a rat by the time I dropped her off, so to ease my conscience, I offered her a lift to work."

Bill laughed. "I don't know how you get away with it, Jake. If I did that, I'd earn myself a broken jaw." He shook his head admiringly.

Greatly relieved at Bill's easy acceptance, Kacie risked a glance over her shoulder. "I wish I'd thought of that," she quipped. She turned to study the bone structure in question. "Although on second thought, best I didn't." She eyed the tough, solid jaw assessingly. "I'd probably have shattered my hand."

"Always provided you'd gotten the chance, Irish," Jake murmured into her ear a few moments later as he escorted her into the restaurant. "I'm a wily street fighter, you know."

Oh, she knew, all right. That was just the trouble.

3

"I THOUGHT I knew most of Atlanta, but I've never been here before," Kacie observed minutes later as she and Bill sat across from Jake at a rustic pine table. Once again the giant had switched roles, becoming the friendly boss lunching with members of his staff. This time Kacie was determined to be as cool as he. She was tired of always being one step behind the maddening man.

Devilry lurked in the midnight eyes as Jake held her gaze, but his voice betrayed nothing but mild interest. "Haven't you?" he queried with a raised brow.

"Jake always knows the best places for food," Bill admitted, joining the conversation.

Kacie glanced appreciatively around the softly lit country-kitchen style dining room. The tables were covered in gaily patterned calico, which made a perfect backdrop for the old-fashioned kerosene lamps and snow-

45

white crockery. If the smells wafting from the plates of the other diners were any indication, the food here had to match the delightful atmosphere.

"Shall we order?" Jake asked.

For a while no one spoke as they studied the menu, which featured everything from homemade chicken soup and buttermilk biscuits to fried pork chops and peach cobbler.

"Now, how did the program work this morning?" Jake asked, all business. He learned back in his chair, his eyes locked on Kacie's face, the pre-lunch drink he'd ordered in one hand.

Kacie sipped her ice water before replying. She sensed Bill's attention. "So far it's been as smooth as silk. No bugs at all. If it continues to prove out, Ted and I should be finished early this afternoon."

"Then we can have a trial run?" Bill questioned.

She nodded.

"Good. Jake has been telling me a little about the problems you ran into with his first plan. I'm glad to hear you got them straightened out so quickly."

"Not quickly," she denied with feeling, responding to Bill's interest.

"I haven't had a chance to go into details," Jake explained, seeing his colleague's avid curiosity. "Why don't you do the honors."

Kacie studied him, half expecting some sign he was mocking her. She hadn't forgotten his comments about her serious attitude, and she knew he hadn't either. He met her gaze, nothing in his expression giving her a clue to his thoughts. She shrugged slightly, then turned to the man at her side.

"You don't mind, do you?" Bill asked when she hesitated.

She smiled slightly. "Not at all. Where would you like me to start?"

"At the beginning," he answered promptly. He then spread his hands apologetically. "I used to be a systems analyst, too. Since Jake kicked me upstairs, I miss it."

Kacie didn't doubt his statement. The grapevine at Weston was very comprehensive on any subject dealing with its wizard owner. She knew that Bill Murphy and Jake had been in college together. She knew also that Bill had been the man chosen to help Jake rebuild the Atlanta plant when it was on the edge of oblivion. The winning combination of Jake's brilliance and Bill's careful attention to detail had begun Weston's meteoric rise in the computer field.

"Okay, step one it is . . ." Kacie launched into a detailed account, which saw them through lunch, leaving Jake to sit back and listen. Occasionally he made a comment to clarify some point. Temporarily repressing her awareness of Jake's dynamic presence, Kacie relaxed as she spoke, knowing Bill saw her only as a quick mind in a field he loved. The waitress arrived to clear the table just as Kacie was winding up her report.

"Three coffees," Jake ordered as she fell silent.

Kacie glanced at him, suddenly realizing how long she'd been talking. She opened her lips to apologize, but a female voice intruded.

"Jake!"

Jake turned his head and caught sight of the woman approaching them. His face creased in a smile of welcome. He rose to his feet. "Abbey," he greeted her, taking her hand and drawing her close for a quick kiss on her smooth cheek.

Kacie saw Bill get to his feet, but her entire attention was focused on the petite female gazing laughingly into

Jake's eyes. She saw the warmth kindle in the black depths as he returned her expression.

"Abigail Stratton, meet Kacie Daniels and Bill Murphy."

Abbey swung friendly brown eyes in their direction. "Hi. I hope I'm not interrupting," she greeted them with a soft midwestern drawl.

"Not at all," Bill assured her with alacrity, his admiration obvious.

Kacie had to admit that the newcomer was definitely pretty enough to merit the many interested male glances she was receiving. She had the sort of soft appeal most men found irresistible. Even her clothes fit the image. Pale cream silk in the form of a classic sleeveless sheath flowed gently over the diminutive but well-endowed figure. She looked cool—and very expensive if the dainty gold-and-green earrings and matching bracelet held real emeralds, as Kacie suspected they did.

Kacie was forced to watch both men hover over the fragile Abbey, seeing that she was seated and finding out if she would join them in having coffee. Kacie gazed from one face to the other, noting their reactions. She might as well have not been there.

"Did you get your luggage moved all right?" Jake asked.

Abbey nodded. "Fortunately. I can't believe my travel agent could have made such a mess," she explained, solicitously including Kacie and Bill in her conversation. "When Uncle Mark thought this trip up on the spur of the moment"—she turned her head to smile at Jake, obviously sharing a private joke—" I had to make some rather hurried arrangements. Naturally, there were repercussions. I arrived and found myself without a bed

for the night, *and* a convention in town." Her expression
was a picture of theatrical disgust, drawing appreciative
chuckles from her male listeners and a weak smile from
Kacie. "Poor Jake. He found me parked on his doorstep,
bags in hand."

"I couldn't turn you out," he agreed with a grin. "Think
what the neighbors and your uncle would have said."

Again there was that secretive look between them.
Kacie took a surreptitious peek at her wristwatch, wishing she could leave. It was increasingly hard to sit across
the table from Jake and this woman who evidently meant
much to him.

"I understand from Jake that you're Mark's hostess
when he gives business dinners," Bill commented.

Abbey nodded. "As you probably know, Uncle Mark
never married. I'm afraid I was the only choice after my
mother died. It has its compensations. I meet a lot of
interesting people. In fact, that's how I met Jake."

Suddenly Kacie realized why Abbey's last name
sounded so familiar. Her uncle's company was the object
of the Chicago merger. Kacie's eyes widened. Hadn't
she heard something about Jake's new love interest during that time? No wonder the two had such a rapport.

"Mr. Weston, if it's all right with you, I think I'd
better be getting back," Kacie interrupted on a carefully
neutral-sounding note. "Ted may have run into some
snags."

A flicker of irritation crossed Jake's face as he, too,
checked the time. "I suppose so." He started to rise.

"No, don't get up," she objected, glancing significantly at his guest. "I can easily take a taxi back."

"We'll both go," Bill decided, following her suggestion. "I've got some work to catch up on also."

Jake eyed Kacie narrowly.

She was surprised at his obvious annoyance. Frankly, she would have thought he would be pleased with her withdrawal. It would give him more time with his *friend*.

"All right," he agreed finally. "I'll stop by at about four."

Kacie nodded before slipping out of her chair. Jake barely seemed to notice her exit as he concentrated on the dark-haired girl at his side. The ride back to Weston was a question-and-answer period for Kacie. Bill used the time to delve into her training background and experience. It was gratifying, at least as far as her career was concerned, but it left her feeling somehow let down. She should have been wildly pleased that she'd achieved the recognition she'd always craved. But she wasn't. The realization disturbed and bewildered her.

The crowning touch to her day was Jake's arrival at the lab at nearly five. She looked up from the first run-through they had just successfully completed.

"Good, I see you started without me," Jake commented, recognizing the printout.

"We had to," Kacie snapped with a pointed glance at the clock. "We'll be late getting out of here as it is."

Jake's expression hardened at her tone, but Kacie didn't give a damn. She was past caring. Because of him her concentration was shot. Even Ted had noticed. She was edgy, and she hated the feeling.

"Now, Kacie, it's not that bad," Ted offered placatingly. "I told you I didn't mind staying late."

Kacie clenched her teeth together on the angry words threatening to erupt. He's the boss, the big boss, she reminded herself desperately.

"I'm sorry," she mumbled. Still Jake said nothing,

simply standing there, seemingly as immovable as a granite boulder.

He finally nodded, the lines in his face softening somewhat. "It's my fault. Too long at lunch." He grinned at Ted.

Kacie stiffened at the oblique mention of Abbey. Jake came over to stand beside her, his eyes on the papers she held.

"May I?" he asked.

She handed them over before turning to her colleague. "Let's run the second set of queries now," she suggested, determined to stick to business.

The results from these were as good as the first set.

"That's it, I think," Kacie observed with a sigh. "Unless you have any more questions...?"

Jake looked up from his study of the last run-through. "No." He turned to Ted. "You can go on home." Ignoring Kacie for the moment, he went back to the papers he held.

She began gathering her things together to leave. She suddenly realized how tired she was. Between her restlessness at night and Jake's upsetting presence during the day, she was exhausted. Thank heavens tomorrow was Saturday. She could sleep in before she had to face packing for the Chicago trip.

"Wait a minute, Kacie." Jake's deep voice stopped her fingers as she unbuttoned her lab coat.

Startled, she glanced over to his seated figure, finding his eyes trained on her. Now she was in for it, she decided, seeing the harsh look on his face. In all fairness, she had to admit she deserved a lecture on her attitude when he came in, especially in view of Ted's presence. She waited for what she was sure would come.

"You look prepared to face a firing squad," Jake observed, eyeing her tense figure. "Why?"

She shrugged, not answering. She would *not* lose her cool this time, she resolved.

Jake studied her silently, speculation in his ebony gaze. "Abbey and I are having Bill over for dinner. She wants you to come, too," he announced, watching her reaction with shrewd eyes.

Her expression must have shown her surprise. "When?" she asked cautiously, silently vowing that an atomic bomb couldn't drive her to accept the invitation.

"Tomorrow night."

She knew he was observing her closely. She stifled the sigh of relief. Short notice, thank the gods. "I have a prior engagement," she declined politely, hesitating a fraction too long.

"Break it," he shot back, obviously recognizing the social lie. Sparks of temper lit his eyes.

"You have no right to demand my weekend!" She stared at him, annoyance rising.

"Worried, Irish?" he taunted, sensing her slipping control.

She glared at him, refusing to swallow his bait.

Midnight eyes clashed with sapphire. For a long moment neither combatant spoke.

"Boss's orders, Irish," Jake commanded with a low growl.

"And if I refuse?" she demanded, anger getting the better of her good sense.

She got her answer in his feral grin. Her job did depend to no small degree on his pleasure—or displeasure—it clearly implied.

For one second she considered telling him to take a

long walk off a short pier. Then sanity returned. Besides, he wasn't propositioning her—just the opposite. Her lashes dropped in defeat. "What time?"

"That's better," he said approvingly. "Bill will pick you up at about seven." He watched her slip off her lab coat and hang it up. His gaze raked the dove-gray dress underneath.

She had her hand on the door when his voice once more halted her progress.

"And, Kacie,"—he paused until she glanced over her shoulder—"No nun outfits. See if you can't dig up something long and sexy."

If looks could kill, Kacie's would have put a sword into his black heart. For a tiny space of time she felt every frustration, every irritation, shining in her angry eyes. In one stride she was through the door, slamming it behind her with a bang that reverberated through the empty corridors. His muffled laughter was the final straw.

"Damn your hide, Jake Weston," she muttered, jamming a rigid finger onto the down button of the elevator panel. "Nun outfits!" Her foot tapped impatiently as she began her slow descent to the ground floor. "Obnoxious . . . overbearing . . . arrogant . . . bully!" She was still muttering epithets for his dictatorial tendencies when the silver panel slid open at the lobby. She hurried across the tiled entryway and shot down the walk to her car.

By morning Kacie's anger had solidified into a cold determination to show Jake Weston just how *un*nunlike she could be. Once again sleep had been an elusive entity. Finally, she had given up entirely and risen with the sun. By seven she had showered, dressed in her jeans and a knit pullover, perched a steaming coffee mug on the end of her dressing table, and assaulted the dark recesses of her closet. One dress after another was ruthlessly hauled out to be just as swiftly discarded in a growing heap on her unmade bed. Many held memories of her days with Michael, but for once she was free of their painful impact. Anger at Jake carried her on a tidal wave that swept away everything in its path.

"Nothing. Not one blasted dress," she muttered, surveying the nearly empty compartment. She picked up her coffee and took a sip. "Ugh!" she groaned, glaring at the cold, dark liquid. Grimacing, she replaced the cup on the vanity with a vicious bang, then glanced around at the havoc she had created.

"It looks like Sherman's march through Georgia," she mumbled, tossing aside a tumbled pile of colored fabrics while hunting for her handbag. When her fingers closed around the smooth leather of her purse, she tugged it free with a cry of triumph. A quick peep inside revealed the presence of her credit cards and a healthy balance in her checkbook. An unholy willfulness imbued her as she headed for the front door. If Jake had been standing there, he would have swallowed his comment on nun outfits.

Kacie's determination carried her through store after store as she sought for *the* dress. She hadn't the foggiest idea what color it was, much less the style, but she knew she wasn't accepting anything less than spectacular even if it took the entire day and her whole bank balance. As the morning wore on, she found much of her anger dissipating as the challenge of finding just the right dress took over. She couldn't help enjoying the compliments paid her by helpful saleswomen as she slipped into creation after designer creation. She even found herself releasing her hair from its restraining band after one particularly chic woman condemned its confinement as criminal. The resulting shiny black cloud had been somehow symbolic of her emergence from her cocoon. She felt as unfettered as the cascade of waves framing her face.

Lunch was a hurried sandwich at a chain hamburger shop, then she was off again. Finally, on a back street in a tiny, narrow little shop, she found *it*.

"Oh, miss, it's stunning!" The breathy gush of the young saleswoman confirmed Kacie's opinion. She stared at the raven-haired stranger in the mirror as she slowly pirouetted.

Deep blue silk shot through with fairy-light silver thread gave a delicate shimmer when it swirled and then clung with each movement of her body. Cut as one piece of fabric, the gown wrapped toward the front in a crossover between high, firm breasts. The ends formed a halter that clasped at the nape of her neck. Tiny hand-sewn tucks radiated from the bodice to the hips in a perfect drape, lovingly accentuating the supple body it covered. With each step Kacie took, the front closure allowed a provocative glimpse of long, slender legs. It was a work of art that only a slim, graceful figure could dare to wear. Kacie had to admit that the effect was dramatic.

"You'll need silver sandals," the girl stated. "A pair with long ties instead of buckles."

Casey grinned, instantly picturing the shoes and *the* dress together. "I think you're right." She laughed in sheer devilry. "Anything else would be a sacrilege," she stated with conviction. "I don't suppose you know where I could find them?" Time was running out, but she meant to finish what she'd started. She felt reckless, free, and wild—and she was loving every minute of it.

Eyes shining, the girl nodded excitedly. "Boy! Do I ever..."

Kacie's exhilaration stayed with her as she luxuriated in her bath before slipping into brand new tiny lace scraps of lingerie. Having chosen her course, she had missed none of the side trips along the way. Kacie Daniels and her working wardrobe were consigned to the computer memory banks for storage.

At last she stood stunningly arrayed in indigo silk, her slender feet wrapped with silver ribbons. Deep sapphire eyes accented with just a hint of blue shadow glowed with pleasure, while delicate cheekbones were highlighted with a flush of anticipation. Kacie skillfully added a touch of rose to her lips and then stepped back for a look at the end result.

"Well, Jake Weston, I hope you like the 'nun' now," she murmured with a wicked wink at her reflection. She had never looked better. It had been worth every penny she'd spent—not only for the dress and shoes, but for the cosmetics as well. She couldn't wait to see Jake's face.

The door chime was timed perfectly. She draped a cobweb-fine shawl of silver around her shoulders, picked up her matching bag, and sailed confidently out of the bedroom, a genuine smile of welcome lighting her face. She opened her door just as the bell pealed again.

"I'm sorry, miss," Bill apologized. "I'm looking for Kacie..." His voice slowly died as his eyes made a sweep of her graceful form, finally settling on her face, his expression a picture of astonishment.

Kacie laughed, a bubbling trill of pure enjoyment. "Am I late?" she asked wickedly, prompted by the same devil of mischief who had been her constant companion since midday.

Bill closed his mouth, which had hung slightly agape, swallowing quickly. "No, just the opposite," he denied in an indistinct voice before clearing his throat.

Taking pity on him, Kacie stood aside. "Would you like to come in for a drink before we go?"

He shook his head. "Jake is expecting us," he replied with a definite air of regret.

Moments later he escorted her to his waiting car. Kacie was conscious of the quick sidelong glances he shot her way. His curiosity was almost palpable.

"Have you known Jake long?" he asked warily.

She turned from her contemplation of the city lights to glance at him. She had almost forgotten his presence in the silence that had prevailed since he'd started the engine. She had been too caught up in the tension building in her as they drew nearer Jake's apartment. The beginnings of panic at his possible reaction had blinded her to Bill's odd reserve.

"No, not long," she answered carefully, studying him for the first time. It was difficult to read his expression in the dim light. She puzzled over his almost uneasy attitude. Where was the colleague of yesterday afternoon? Had her altered appearance been the cause of his drastic change? She could see him turning over her reply in his mind.

"What do you think of Abbey?"

Kacie's eyes widened slightly in surprise. "She's very lovely," she observed honestly.

He nodded. "Isn't she? Nice, too," he added in an almost defiant tone.

Her lips twitched with amusement. He sounded as

though he were daring her to deny it. "Yes," she agreed, wondering what else he expected her to say on the basis of one short meeting.

"We're here," he announced, drawing Kacie's attention to the soaring condominium directly ahead. He stopped at the guard house of the front entrance, gave their names, and then waited while the security man checked his sheet of visitors due before calling ahead to announce their arrival.

When the scrolled iron gates swung open into the complex, Kacie marveled at the beautiful surroundings and the vast wealth so many precautions protected. Suddenly she doubted the wisdom of confronting Jake on his own home ground. The urge to retreat before he saw her in her new guise was swiftly becoming undeniable. She had been a fool, she acknowledged as she allowed Bill to help her from the car. Jake was accustomed to sophisticated women from glamorous backgrounds, no matter what his own beginnings had been. She might look the part, but she certainly couldn't act it. "Irish" and all her temperament were submerged under Miss Daniels's logic and common sense. But it was too late to retreat. They were standing in front of the penthouse door. The muted peal of melodic bells came from within as Bill released the ornate door pull.

Committed now, Kacie fixed a smile on her face as the panel swung open. Expecting to be met by Jake, she was disconcerted to find herself staring down at the top of Abbey's dark head. She quickly lowered her gaze to meet Abbey's friendly grin.

"Come in, you two," the younger woman commanded cheerfully. "Jake's on the phone. You know the way, I'm sure, Bill, so why don't you get Kacie some wine while I show her where to lay her wrap." She glanced up at her. "It is all right if I call you Kacie, isn't it?" she asked with unselfconscious ease and warmth.

Kacie nodded, feeling some of her trepidation melt away. Abbey's all-embracing smile would have put even the most nervous person at ease. Kacie liked her, she realized. She followed her into a luxurious lime-green-and-white bedroom, which could only be the guest room, and slipped her shawl from her shoulders.

"What a stunning dress!" Abbey exclaimed. "Turn around so I can see the back."

Obligingly, Kacie slowly pirouetted until she was once again facing Abbey.

Abbey sighed ruefully. "I couldn't wear a gown like that in a million years," she murmured without a trace of jealousy.

Kacie eyed Abbey's petite figure, knowing she spoke the truth. The simple lines of the soft yellow silk she wore were much more suited for her diminutive build. The classic princess cut lent her the illusion of height, yet didn't overpower her. "I love what you're wearing," she offered sincerely.

Kacie was surprised at the tinge of pink that crept along Abbey's cheeks. The dark-brown eyes glowed with pleasure. "No wonder Jake likes you," Abbey smiled.

"Hey, are you two going to come out, or shall I bring the glasses in there?" Bill's voice sounded from the direction of the living room.

"We'd better go," Abbey decided with a grin.

Bill had their drinks waiting as they entered. Kacie took a seat at one end of an overstuffed ivory sofa, with Abbey taking the place beside her, leaving Bill to return to the cinnamon wingback chair across from them. Their wine stood on the low glass table between them.

Abbey glanced across the room to the closed door before turning her attention to her guests. "Jake shouldn't be much longer. My uncle is usually brief and to the point."

"How long are you staying?" Bill asked with obvious interest.

Abbey shrugged. "Until Jake goes back, probably. I hate traveling alone unless there's no other alternative."

Warnings sounded in Kacie's mind. She mustn't for a moment forget about the attachment between Abbey and Jake, no matter how friendly the young woman was. Wanting to force Jake to acknowledge her as a woman and interfering in a relationship were two entirely different matters. While she definitely didn't mind taking Jake down a peg or so, poaching was not on her agenda.

"Have you been here before?" Bill questioned Abbey.

"No, this is my first and probably my last time," she replied with a rueful grin.

Kacie watched as Bill's reserve melted in the glow of Abbey's gentle charm. It didn't bother her in the least that the two of them appeared to have momentarily forgotten her. She found her eyes drawn against her will to the closed door. She looked away almost immediately, concentrating on Bill and Abbey.

"Jake tells me you're a systems analyst," Abbey commented, drawing Kacie into the conversation.

Kacie's lashes flickered briefly at the realization that Jake had discussed her with his girlfriend. "That's right."

Abbey didn't seem to notice the terseness of her reply. "Have you been with Weston Technology long?"

"About four months. Before that I worked for Comco," she returned, anticipating the question.

Abbey sighed. "It must be fascinating work. Jake

explained a bit about the system you two devised. I confess I lost him after the first three sentences."

Bill chuckled indulgently. "Don't worry about it. Most people get lost when Jake climbs onto his pet hobbyhorse. Sometimes I swear he breathes computers."

Struck by the flirtatious note in his voice, Kacie stared at him from beneath her lashes. She thought he was Jake's friend, yet he was making no secret of his interest in Abbey.

While Kacie was musing on Bill's odd behavior, the door on the far side of the room opened, admitting Jake.

"Sorry to be so long," he apologized, quickly striding across the thick dark brown carpet and stopping at the bar to fix himself a drink.

"Is everything all right?" Bill asked.

He nodded with his back to them, then turned, gesturing with his hand. "Anyone need a refill while I'm here?" His eyes flickered briefly over Bill and Abbey before settling on Kacie's composed face.

Kacie's eyes met his across the space separating them. As though they were invisibly linked, she physically felt him register the change in her. She watched his ebony stare narrow before he boldly surveyed her figure, leaving her feeling shaken and breathless. The hand holding her wine glass trembled slightly when she carried it to her lips, but she forced herself to control the quivers. She would not let him see how much power he wielded with just a look. Oh, for the anonymity of her other self. Miss Daniels never would have elicited such a blatant appraisal.

"Well, well, I never would have recognized you," he growled with apparent admiration. "What happened to the computer lady, Kacie?"

Kacie fought down the pink flush his teasing rumble

evoked. "I gave her the night off," she murmured with mock sweetness.

"It looks more like an entire week," he replied outrageously.

Kacie glared helplessly at his grinning face. She didn't know whom she was more annoyed with—herself for precipitating his reaction, or him for taking advantage of her.

"Jake, you're embarrassing Kacie. That's not nice," Abbey scolded, unexpectedly coming to Kacie's aid. "I think her dress is fabulous."

Jake raised his glass in salute. "So do I, surprisingly enough. But I think what's in it is even better."

Abbey's gasp was covered by Bill's masculine chuckle. No one but Jake appeared to notice the temper sparkling in Kacie's eyes.

"At least you recognized her, which is more than I did," Bill added wryly.

Kacie leaned forward to place her empty glass on the coffee table. She felt safer with the fragile missile out of her hands. It wouldn't do to fling the exquisite goblet at her irritating host.

She was aware of Jake moving toward her. He stopped at her side as she leaned back against the cushions, her eyes fixed on his face.

His lips twitched at her expression. "Move over, Irish," he commanded, reinforcing his order with an insistent nudge from one muscular leg.

Unable to think of a good excuse not to do as he asked, Kacie reluctantly slid closer to Abbey.

"What a lovely nickname," Abbey commented innocently. "Does it have any special significance?"

"My ancestry," Kacie hurried to explain, with a furtive

sidelong peek at the man by her side. She didn't for one second trust the dark gleam in his eyes. He was bent on teasing her, it seemed, regardless of Abbey's presence. She found herself strangely angered by his apparent callous disregard for the younger woman's feelings. He had a reputation for ruthless determination in business, but somehow she hadn't expected that part of his personality to carry over into his private life. Especially not with someone like Abbey. She was too sweet to warrant such treatment.

Abbey laughed in rueful self-mockery. "I should have guessed from your coloring and your name."

Jake shifted his position, extending his arm along the back of the sofa, behind Kacie's head. "Those aren't the only things she inherited."

Kacie inhaled sharply. If he so much as mentioned her temper, he was going to get a front-row seat for the biggest explosion in Altanta's colorful history, she vowed silently. As she sensed his growing amusement, her anger rose. He was laughing at her, and they both knew it. And there wasn't a thing she could do about it without making a scene. Caught up in her feelings of helplessness, Kacie barely heard Bill join the conversation.

"Heredity is a funny thing. My people were all farmers, yet I don't have a bit of interest in the country. On the other hand, Jake here was born and raised in the city, and he now prefers what we'd call old-fashioned country livin'," he remarked, apparently oblivious to Jake's veiled taunts.

Abbey nodded. "I know what you mean. When my parents died, leaving me with only my uncle, he was so sure I would come around to taking part in the family business. But I couldn't. I don't have the least aptitude for figures." She sighed before smiling slightly. "When he realized that his expectations in my direction were doomed, he turned his efforts to finding me a mate capable of handling the company."

She glanced across Kacie to Jake, her lips quirking into a mischievous grin. "Poor Uncle Mark. He'd have a fit if he knew how badly his plans were going."

Kacie couldn't control her start of surprise or the questioning look on her face.

Noticing her expression, Abbey giggled, looking more like a child than a grown woman. "We fooled you, too, didn't we?"

"She's not the only one," Bill observed with a faint tinge of annoyance. He glanced at his friend.

Jake shrugged lazily. "You'd better finish what you started, Abbey, since you've gone this far. Bill, for one, appears very interested."

Abbey grimaced artistically before spreading her hands in defeat. If she noticed the slightly embarrassed look on Bill's intent face, she gave no sign of it as she addressed herself to Kacie.

"Uncle Mark is a bit on the managing side," she began slowly, drawing a barely smothered choke of laughter from Jake. She shot him an amused glare before continuing. "He's a pet, really, but he's sure I need a husband and that the company needs a young man. He thinks he's found them both in Jake." For a moment Abbey's gentle face took on an almost fierce expression. "He simply wouldn't listen when I tried to tell him Jake was just a friend, so I had to resort to bending the truth a little."

"What she means is she let Mark think there was more between us than there was, planning to tell him later that it hadn't worked out," Jake elaborated. "With the merger completed, I'd be out of range of Mark's planning, and Abbey would be free from the pressure of marrying in order to provide the company with what Mark considers a suitable leader."

Bill appeared as astonished as Kacie felt. Relief at the true situation vied with the questions she was dying to ask. Fortunately, Bill wasn't so reticent.

"So what are you doing in Atlanta, Abbey? Surely that's not promoting your ultimate goal?" His voice was a clear indicator of his skepticism.

Kacie glanced at Jake, curious to see how he was reacting to his friend's blunt questions. Catching her eye, he grinned. "I told her she should've stood up for her rights, but she wouldn't listen."

"Well! I like that, Jake Weston! Uncle Mark was badgering you just as much as he was me," Abbey retorted inelegantly. She looked to Bill for defense. "You want to know what I'm doing here? My dear, darling uncle sent me here on some flimsy excuse, that's what," she finished in disgust.

"Shall I serve dinner now, sir?"

The soft query startled them all, instantly silencing further discussion.

"Good idea, Dawes." Jake placed his empty glass on the table beside Kacie's, then rose. "Bill, since I'm in the doghouse at the moment, why don't you take Abbey in?"

Jake held out his hand to Kacie, an eyebrow arched at her brief hesitation. "For a minute there I thought Miss Daniels was back," he murmured for her ears alone.

Kacie smiled sweetly, her blue eyes gleaming with challenge. "Oh, no, Jake, she's still out . . . temporarily."

Jake's deep-throated laughter echoed in the dining

room as he pulled out a chair for her on his right. Bill and Abbey broke off their conversation in mid-sentence.

"What's the joke?" Bill asked curiously, evidently noting Jake's amusement and the slight flush on Kacie's face.

Kacie veiled her eyes, mentally damning her wayward tongue. She wished there were a nearby dark hole in which she could hide. Why couldn't she resist the temptation to cross verbal swords with a man like Jake Weston? She stiffened, feeling Jake's fingers trail lightly across her bare shoulders, sending ripples of sensation coursing through her.

"I never noticed what a long nose you have, my friend," Jake responded.

Kacie released the breath she had been unconsciously holding. She glanced at her host as he took his place beside her. For a moment her eyes were liquid with relief and gratitude for his evasive answer. She was surprised at the warmth reflected in his ebony gaze. Black as the darkest velvet, it reached out to stroke her in a visual caress, and she shuddered with pleasure.

Bill shrugged amicably, not in the least abashed by Jake's comment. He took his seat at the other end of the table. "I should have known better than to ask you anything."

Bill's slow drawl intruded on Kacie's consciousness, abruptly shattering the strange hold of Jake's hypnotic stare. She dragged her eyes free of him to glance across the table. The need to deny the force of Jake's physical attraction made her reach for her cloak of composure like a security blanket. Faking a calm she didn't feel, she sought a safe, impersonal topic.

"How are you liking Atlanta, Abbey?" She risked a

quick peek at Jake. There was a definite gleam of amusement now in place of the earlier warmth. She stifled the urge to childishly poke out her tongue and add "so there." It was too bad she couldn't maintain a suitably serious expression while she listened to Abbey extol the virtues of the fair city—but how was she to know the maddening man would brazenly wink at her obvious ploy while Abbey chattered.

Dinner was a delight, starting with luscious jumbo shrimp iced to perfection. The succulent filets mignons that followed were cooked to mouth-watering tenderness. The deep ruby wine chosen as an accompaniment sparkled in crystal goblets, echoing the rich crimson of the roses adorning the center of the table.

From her position opposite a huge picture window, Kacie had a panoramic view of downtown Atlanta in all its splendor. The twinkling lights of the streets and shops were in vivid contrast to the chandelier, which cast a muted glow over the dark mahogany table and the delicate porcelain and crystal gracing its surface. The robin's-egg blue walls brought the freedom of the open sky to the room, denying it its penthouse dimensions.

Jake had abandoned his teasing manner, much to Kacie's relief. Exuding a charm she found impossible to resist, he was the epitome of an excellent host.

Somehow it became easy for her to relax and enjoy the conversation flowing around her. Jake was a brilliant man, his range of interests far-reaching. Although Bill was clearly not his friend's equal in quickness, he carried an amazing amount of knowledge in his head. But Abbey was the real surprise as far as Kacie was concerned. While she obviously couldn't hope to compete with the men in their business experience, she had an uncanny ability to slice through the bewildering details of an issue and go right to the heart of it. This was especially obvious in the case of politics—one field about which Kacie freely admitted she knew exactly zero. Consequently, the present debate was being conducted without her.

"I tell you it won't work," Bill insisted, his clenched hand thudding against the table to emphasize his point.

Abbey eyed him calmly, apparently unmoved by the masculine pronouncement. "Why not?"

For a moment he looked nonplussed, before rallying, "Because it's not feasible."

Kacie's lips twitched at his evasive answer.

"What do you want to bet she wins?" Jake murmured against Kacie's hair, causing her to give a startled little jump.

She looked at him, her breath catching in her throat at his nearness. His face was only inches from hers, the lines of experience, laughter, and character etched plainly across his rugged features. For a moment his life lay like an open book before her discerning eyes. The triumphs, the failures, the joys, and the sorrows were recorded in its hollows and planes. She had the strangest need to trace the tiny fans at the corners of each eye, the deep grooves carved below his cheekbones. Her mouth went dry with the force of her emotions. In the distance she could hear the rise and fall of Abbey's ongoing battle. Her tongue darted out to moisten her lips.

"What is it?" he demanded quietly. The amused note was gone from his voice. "Tell me what you're think-ing . . . now . . . this minute," he commanded with an odd urgency.

Kacie shook her head in mute denial. She couldn't. It was madness. "I can't," she whispered breathlessly.

Something flickered briefly in his eyes, then it was gone. "You won't always be able to escape me, Irish." He leaned back in his chair, picking up his wine glass, his gaze still holding hers. "One day that shell of yours won't be the protection you think it is."

His faintly derisive tone was just the stimulus Kacie needed. "My 'shell,' as you call it, is my own, Jake Weston," she retorted in an angry undertone. "Its function is not open to conjecture by you."

"That's putting me in my place, Irish," he approved, openly laughing at her.

Kacie glared at him, resenting his mockery. But before she could voice the angry epithets churning in her brain, Bill intervened.

"Don't tell me you lost out, too, Jake?"

Devilry was back in his eyes. "I admit I lost the battle, but the war's not over yet."

"Don't count on it, Jake, my friend," Abbey remarked with a decided burst of feminine satisfaction. She glanced at Kacie's determined face. "I think you might have met your match."

Kacie smiled at her unexpected ally. "If I recall my history right, one battle is all it takes," she said pointedly. She turned to stare at Jake, defiance that only he could know in every line of her body. "The final one."

"Yes, but who's to know which one that is?" was his cryptic answer.

4

KACIE REMEMBERED JAKE'S comment all too clearly two hours later when she found herself accepting his escort home. Seconds after Bill had offered to take Abbey back to her hotel, Kacie had realized that Jake had intended this all evening. She had wondered at the way he automatically seemed to pair off Bill and Abbey. She had thought at first he sensed a budding relationship between his quieter friend and the gentle dark-haired woman. Now Kacie wasn't so sure of his motives. She stared at him in the dim light of the Mercedes' interior, suspicion growing steadily within her.

"Why?" she asked bluntly.

Jake's fingers relaxed their hold on the key he had just inserted in the ignition. He turned, casually regarding her with a faint smile. He didn't pretend to miss her meaning. "You wouldn't have allowed me to drive you home otherwise," he stated calmly, his eyes strangely intent on hers.

"And the dinner—was that a trick, too?" she demanded, feeling as though the enemy were closing in on her vulnerable flanks. Why hadn't she held to her refusal? If she had, she would be home, safe from the maneuverings of Jake's superior forces. Had she foolishly believed she could outwit such a man? She should have known better.

"It was no trick, Kacie," Jake quietly rebuked. "I don't need to resort to those tactics." One large hand covered her clenched fingers, his thumb roving slowly over the tense muscles until they relaxed in his warm grasp. "I wanted to see you, to have dinner with you. Is that such a crime?"

She shook her head, confused by the coaxing words. The soft rasp of his voice was curiously soothing in the cocoon of darkness surrounding them. "I don't understand, Jake," she whispered, bewilderment evident in her husky admission. "Why me?"

He leaned closer until his broad shoulders blocked out the muted illumination of the parking area lanterns.

Kacie's senses came tinglingly alive at the woodsy fragrance of his cologne, the warm, male scent of his skin. She stared at him, her eyes wide. "I've never met anyone like you," she murmured, scarcely aware that she had spoken her thoughts aloud. "What do you want of me?"

"Don't you know, Kacie?" he asked. He raised his hand to her bare throat, gently shackling the smooth white column with his fingers.

"No," she denied, the knowledge growing in her. "No!"

Jake smiled, a slow, devastating grin of wisdom and worldly experience. "Liar," he chided softly.

Kacie stared at him, knowing she should draw away

or at least resist, yet powerless to do either. He was going to kiss her, she knew. His intention was written in his eyes, but she could no more evade the descent of his lips than she could stop breathing.

The first touch of his mouth was gentle—a request for her response, not a demand. Therein lay Kacie's defeat. The force she had instinctively braced herself to meet was absent. Off balance and disarmed by the low-key approach, she was left with nothing to fight. As his tongue lightly traced the outline of her lips, she sighed. "Please, Jake," she pleaded against his skin.

"Please what, Irish?" he murmured, his lips nibbling along her jaw to the sensitive hollow at the base of her ear. "Don't you like what I'm doing?"

She freed her hands to push away the wide chest pressing her against the plush leather seat. "Yes...I mean no..." she mumbled. "Stop it!" Her command was little more than a gasping bid for freedom.

"Why, Kacie? Is Irish getting restless?" he taunted, his voice a low rumble in her ear.

She heard his words, but the sense of them was lost under the seductive quality of his caress. The hand around her throat had begun a slow sensual massage that was sending quivers of pleasure through her body. She moaned as she sank deeper into the cloud of feelings he was creating. The hands vainly seeking her release stilled, then slowly inched upward until they found Jake's broad shoulders, the nails finding purchase in the expensive silk suit.

"That's right, Irish, hold me," Jake murmured just before he claimed her lips.

Pliant, her mouth softly yielding, Kacie was effectively silenced by his kiss. Never had she known such raw intensity, such deep excitement. Reeling under the strength of it, she responded mindlessly, blindly opening her lips to the probing search of his tongue. Senses blurred, completely overwhelmed, she gave herself up to the moment. Their bodies, touching so closely, were almost one. She felt Jake's heartbeats as her own, and the heavy rasp of his breathing set the rhythm of their embrace. His hands flowed over her sensitive skin, caressing first her throat, then trailing down the pale valley between her breasts. She caught her breath as his fingers slipped beneath the skimpy halter of her gown and into her bra in a tantalizing invasion. When he cupped one satiny mound in its lacy veil, she moaned softly in delicious torment. For a moment, time ceased its relentless march.

Then it was over. Her lips were free, her breath coming in tiny gasps between their swollen fullness. The silky fabric of her dress replaced Jake's possessive touch on her breast. She opened passion-drugged eyes to stare into his face. She felt a rosy flush run under her skin at the desire she saw mirrored in the velvety depths of his gaze. Her lashes drifted down to block out his image. She was suddenly unutterably weary. She was defenseless.

"I'll take you home."

She opened her eyes. "Home?" she repeated as though she had never heard the word.

Jake nodded, the ebony gaze once again impenetrable. "You look all in." He released her slowly, almost reluctantly. "Why don't you shut your eyes and relax. We'll be there before you know it."

Kacie was bewildered by the impersonal kindness in the low growl. Had the last few moments been a dream, she wondered dazedly. More exhausted than she'd thought, she succumbed to the temptation of doing exactly what Jake had suggested. She was barely aware of his starting the car. It seemed like only seconds passed before a draft of cool air invaded her warm resting place. She opened drowsy eyes to see Jake standing over her in the darkness. Hadn't she seen him thus before, she mused fuzzily.

"Come on, computer lady," Jake teased softly as he reached for her arm to help her from the car.

Swaying slightly, Kacie stood up.

"Shall I carry you?"

She shook her head, the cold night air rapidly dispelling the mists of sleep.

He took her hand, unobtrusively guiding her up the walk. "Pity."

"That depends on your point of view," she replied, unable to resist retaliating. Somehow she realized she was safe . . . for the moment. How she knew, she had no idea. But she did.

Minutes later, she leaned against her door, listening to the measured tread of Jake's footsteps retreating down the hall. The gentle, almost chaste, kiss he had placed on her lips still lingered. She raised her hand and lightly traced their fullness, which had so recently known his possession. Baffled, she shook her head at the paradox of his behavior. Why hadn't he pressed the advantage he had over her? It would have been so easy, she admitted to herself. Why had he held back?

She headed for her bedroom, still pondering Jake's curious behavior. By the time she slipped between the lavender sheets that echoed the paler shade of her bedroom walls, she had no answer. But nothing, not even Jake, had the power to disturb her sleep this night. The days of exhausting after-hours work, the last few nights of restlessness, the hectic afternoon of shopping, and, most of all, the draining emotional seesaw prompted by Jake's presence finally took their toll. Kacie was asleep almost from the moment her head touched the pillow.

She awoke, renewed, to the golden rose of early dawn. Stretching lazily, she peered at her bedside clock. She blinked in surprise at the early hour. Six o'clock. Usually she slept in on Sunday, although during her school years she had always risen with the sun. Of course, then she'd had her horse, Navajo. Those had been secure times, happy times in a lovely home with a loving family. Images of the redwood fences stretching across lush fields rose in her mind. She could almost feel the wind singing through her hair and whipping Navajo's mane against her face as together they soared over the jumps her father had so painstakingly erected.

She slid from her bed, remembering the pleasure of watching the birth of a new day from horseback and inhaling the clean smell of dewy grass. Suddenly she had an overwhelming longing to recapture those moments. Navajo was long gone, but there was still her longtime friend, Jan, who worked out at Stone Mountain's stable.

Before she could change her mind, Kacie quickly dialed her old school chum. In a matter of minutes she had hung up the phone, a smile of pleasure and anticipation curving her lips. After making a lightning swift change into well-worn denims, a long-sleeved cotton plaid shirt, and her riding boots—which were, naturally, buried in a back corner of her closet—she stopped by the kitchen for an apple, a chocolate bar, and a carrot for Jan's mare.

The roads were nearly deserted as Kacie accelerated up the ramp to Interstate 20, where she could later join I-285 to Stone Mountain Park. The famous attraction was one of Kacie's favorite places. Although not large—boasting only 3,800 acres—when judged against some other U.S. parks, it was home for the world's biggest granite mountain. On the face of that mighty gray mass were carved the figures of Jefferson Davis, the president of the Confederacy, and generals Robert E. Lee and Stonewall Jackson.

Awe inspiring as the huge sculpture was, at the moment Kacie was more interested in the peace and solitude of the twelve miles of wooded trails winding around its base.

A little less than an hour later she pulled to a stop in the red-clay parking area near the stables. She glanced around the beautifully kept paddocks, searching for Jan's carroty curls. Seeing only the sleek, multicolored coats of the horses, she opened the car door and got out, pausing to collect the tan pullover sweater she had brought along to ward off the early morning chill.

"Hey, Kacie, over here!"

Following the sound of the greeting, Kacie saw her friend in the far paddock. Waving her hand to signal she'd heard, Kacie headed in Jan's direction. As she got closer, she ran her eyes expertly over a steel-dust mare, whose reins were tied to the top rail of the enclosure.

"She's a beauty, Jan," she offered admiringly. "Arab?"

"Purebred," her proud owner elaborated. "I got her last summer."

Kacie's eyes widened in surprise. "Has it been that long since we've seen each other?"

Jan reached for the bridle, then led the mare through

the open gate. "Sure has. Doesn't seem like it, does it?"

"No, it doesn't. Jan, I can't take . . ." She paused, not knowing the horse's name.

"Delight." Jan grinned at Kacie's expression. "Weird, isn't it? The girl I bought her from named her. I was going to change it—until I rode her." She passed the reins to Kacie. "As far as riding her is concerned, you'd be doing me a favor. One of the stable hands is out sick, and I don't have time today to take her out."

Kacie was still uncertain. She knew how hard her friend had worked and saved to buy the long-desired Arabian. "You're sure?"

Jan nodded. "Of course, you dope. I was around when you won all those ribbons, remember?" She patted the mare's dark, glossy neck affectionately. "Just don't get too fond of her, 'cause even for you she's not for sale."

Kacie grinned, reassured. "Okay," she agreed before swinging lightly into the saddle. "If I'm not back before lunch, send out a search party."

Jan's laughter was drowned out by the thumping of Delight's hooves as Kacie urged the mare into a slow trot toward the open field beyond the stable. Within a few minutes Kacie knew what Jan had meant about the horse's name. Delight had a smooth, even gait and the beautiful manners of a well-trained animal. Kacie reached forward to pat the satiny neck. At her urging the Arab broke into a rocking canter that stirred the air to a light breeze, lifting Kacie's hair like feathers in the wind.

As the deep green grass gave way to trees and the beginnings of the path she remembered, Kacie slowed her mount. Moving deeper into the thickening forest, she found the tranquillity she'd been seeking. Here, where towering green sentinels reached for the heavens, where the only sounds were birdsong, the muted thud of Delight's hooves on the leaf-carpeted trail, and the creak of leather, she felt at peace.

Now she was ready to think about Jake, to be objective about her reactions to him. Subconsciously she knew this was why she had come. So much had happened in so little time. She knew beyond any doubt that she couldn't go to Chicago with Jake until she had come to terms with what was happening to her.

All of her life she had been a loner, partly because she was an only child, but also because her intelligence had made a normal childhood so difficult for her. In grammar school, where most children had playmates, she'd had very few. Her braininess had been a stumbling block for the budding maturity of her male classmates, while her looks had been a source of envy for the members of her own sex. Those early years had taught her to hide her feelings behind a mask of cool reserve. Only with her parents had she felt truly free to be herself. When they died, there had been no one close except for Jan, who had been her friend since tenth grade. Then came Michael.

He had entered her life at her most vulnerable time. In him she had thought she'd finally found someone she could love and be loved and accepted by in return. What a fool she had been. After his betrayal, she had promised herself she wouldn't allow anyone else to touch her again. She had reckoned without Jake.

The ring of steel on stone broke into her thoughts, focusing her eyes on the scene in front of her. The park's lake lay like a shimmering jewel amid the emerald velvet of the trees lining its white sand beaches. The huge silver-gray granite mountain loomed on the far shore, its rough textures visible even from her distance. Enthralled with the view, Kacie dismounted, tethering Delight to a low-hanging pine branch. She moved a few feet away and sat down, her back braced against a tree trunk and her legs stretched out in front of her. She rested her head against the crumbling bark behind her, her eyes glued to the mountain.

Older than the mighty Himalayas, it rose like a giant above the earth. Worn, battered by nature's fury and the carvings of men, it still stood as a monument of strength.

In many ways Jake was like that granite. Strong, deeply etched by his background and his drive to succeed, his face, too, bore the scars of his passage through time. And like the mountain, he commanded respect. He stood high above those mortals who shared his world. The power of his presence was not to be ignored.

And now he wanted her; that was obvious.

But did she want *him?* That was the question.

Physically, she admitted, he attracted her immensely. But for her that was not enough. Basically she was too old-fashioned to enter into a casual sexual relationship, which was all Jake appeared to want. She had the feeling he was slowly and inevitably driving her closer to his bed. Somehow he had found the key to her defenses. Every time she lost her temper, he gained another inch. She was losing the control she had always prized, and she couldn't afford to. Jake was a determined opponent, and she needed every weapon at her command to defeat him.

No matter what, she must guard against losing her temper. It didn't take much intelligence to guess that Jake deliberately needled her for just that reason. He was at his worst in regard to her mode of dress.

A wicked smile curved her lips as a diabolical idea occurred to her. She would change her image a bit. Not with things as dramatic as the blue gown, but definitely with attractive and colorful clothes. And she would begin with the Chicago trip. Knowing Jake, she could bet that whatever free time she had he would try to appropriate. She needed some excuse—a real one this time, not like the social evasion she had fabricated for the dinner party. What could be more natural than taking advantage of the shopping offered by a city like Chicago? It would serve a dual purpose, keeping her out of Jake's way—after all, what man likes picking out a woman's clothes—plus depriving him of the opportunity to compare what she wore to a nun's habit. And since she hadn't ever been to the "Windy City" before, she could add sightseeing to her list of solo activities.

"There, Jake Weston, let's see you top that," she challenged aloud, her eyes on the mountain.

Suddenly ravenously hungry, she dug into her pocket for the apple and the candy bar she'd brought with her. She munched happily on the fruit, then the chocolate. Having a battle plan made all the difference in her attitude toward the impending trip.

All she had to do was remain calm when they met, which would be only during business hours if her scheme worked. Difficult as it might be, she knew she could handle that much.

She had her first chance to test her resolve the next morning when the doorbell pealed, announcing Jake's arrival.

"You're early," she greeted him with a faint, cool smile.

He grinned, a flicker of genuine amusement in his eyes. "Only a little. Maybe I was hoping to catch you looking less than your usual efficient self," he admitted, eyeing her trim figure.

Ignoring his comment, she shrugged in apparent unconcern and stepped back so he could enter. She knew very well what the dark brown tailored suit didn't do for her. It fit well enough to have been attractive if the somber shade had had even the smallest touch of life, which it didn't.

She gestured toward the single large case beside the door. "I didn't think you'd appreciate waiting," she replied evenly as she collected her handbag. "I'm ready."

Jake glanced questioningly at the solitary piece of luggage. "Is this all you're taking?" he demanded as he picked it up.

She nodded. "I've decided to take advantage of the trip to shop for some new clothes," she explained, purposefully giving her attention to the search for her door keys, which were, as usual, at the bottom of her purse. She intended to let him know he wasn't the only one capable of making plans.

"Good." The brief word held a wealth of masculine satisfaction.

Kacie's head lifted sharply, one hand gripping her keys. She saw the triumph lurking in his ebony gaze. The urge to tell him he wasn't the one responsible for her new interest in clothes was strong—at least not in the way he obviously thought. Only her vow to remain calm stopped her—that and the fact that she could see him waiting for some reply.

"Shall we go?" she asked instead.

For a moment, she was sure he would comment. He

didn't, although there was a distinctly mocking gleam in his eyes that made her itch to let fly.

"Are you nervous, or have you retreated back into that shell of yours?"

Kacie turned, startled out of her study of Atlanta International, the second-largest airport in the United States. "Neither," she answered briefly, allowing her eyes to catch and hold Jake's skeptical look. Since she had gotten into the car, she had managed to retain her poise by keeping her replies to the questions Jake threw at her brief. She had ignored the underlying meanings that peppered most of his conversation. He appeared intent on provoking some sort of reaction from her, while she was equally determined not to let him achieve his goal. She sensed his impatience with her before they had traveled more than a few miles from her apartment. Until now the resulting silence that had fallen between them had been total.

"Whatever it is, it had better stop," he warned as he swung the Mercedes into the private parking area. Kacie knew he planned to leave the car for one of the staff to pick up later.

"What shall we talk about?" she questioned, all reasonableness. She tried to convey the picture of the perfect employee confronting a demanding boss. She saw his face tighten as his jaw clenched in rising annoyance.

A tiny twitch of her lips gave away the humor she felt at his obvious frustration.

"Suddenly you're awfully brave, Kacie Daniels," he growled. "I wonder what you'd do if I took you up on that challenge?"

Kacie's eyes widened, no doubt betraying her agitation as she realized the seriousness of his last words. She felt she was facing a big hungry cat, whose switching tail and low grumble held the threat of an immediate meal—her. Blast her wayward tongue. And she was so sure she could handle Jake. Hah! Only with a gun, whip, and chair—and at least two states between them.

The great leonine head nodded, apparently satisfied with her speechless state. "I didn't think you were ready for that." He paused, watching as she slipped quickly out of the car. "Yet," he added in a softly voiced threat.

After dropping his verbal bomb, Jake didn't make any attempt to follow up his temporary advantage—something for which Kacie was very grateful. His jet was waiting for them at the small private terminal adjacent to the huge structure for the jumbo commercial aircraft.

This was Kacie's first flight in an executive plane. She wasn't sure whether she was worried or not. Normally, she preferred to do her traveling by car, only resorting to the skies when time and distance made it absolutely necessary. She eyed the sleek, gleaming hull of the Lear Longhorn as they approached the boarding steps. She knew from the feature articles about Jake in the trade magazines what the Lear's model and year were, and she even had a mental layout of the custom interior. What she hadn't gleaned from her study was a concept of its size. It was smaller than she'd imagined. Just as she was about to place her foot on the first silver grid, she hesitated for a fraction of a second. She heard Jake come to an abrupt halt behind her to avoid bumping into her.

"Anything wrong?" he asked close to her ear.

She shook her head, not about to divulge her niggling doubts about his expensive machine. "No, nothing." She slowly mounted the stairs, automatically ducking her head as she boarded.

She couldn't suppress a gasp of admiration for the interior. Deep cinnamon shag carpet stretched beneath her feet to the rear of the plane. Although it was obviously designed for work as well as comfort, the flying suite was beautifully appointed. Along one wall was a sofa, complete with overstuffed pale blue cushions and flanked by mahogany end tables. Across from that was an executive-size desk and chair. A bar outfitted with a small refrigerator and backed by mirrors reflecting crystal glasses in clear, enclosed shelves stretched across the rear of the craft, ending at a door that Kacie guessed led to the bathroom/shower combination.

"Welcome aboard." A cheerful male voice drew her attention from her surroundings.

She smiled weakly at the man in uniform emerging from the cockpit.

"Kacie, this is our captain, Tony Markham. Tony, Kacie Daniels." Jake turned to the man. "Ready?"

Tony grinned. "You bet, boss."

"We'll sit here until after takeoff," Jake directed, gesturing toward a pair of captain's chairs.

Obediently, Kacie took the place he indicated by the window and fastened her seat belt. Almost immediately she felt the jet begin to move. She licked her dry lips nervously, her fingers tightening slightly on the padded armrests. The touch of Jake's hand on hers broke her mesmerized study of the ground rolling past. She turned to him, her eyes evidently showing the apprehension she felt.

"I never would have believed it," Jake teased gently. "Why didn't you tell me you were afraid of flying?"

She smiled weakly. "It's not something I'm very proud of."

"Well, don't let it get to you," he grinned back. "Put me in a room with one bee and I turn into a raving maniac."

"I'll bet," Kacie challenged skeptically.

He nodded. "It's true. Once when I was a kid our school took a field trip to a farm. The owner liked honey, so he kept his own hive. Being a naturally inquisitive little brat"—he paused in his recital to gather her rigid fingers in his as the plane began to turn toward the runway—"I decided I wanted a look at how the stuff was made. Being a city kid, I figured all I had to do was lift the lid and take a quick peek, and no one would be the wiser."

Caught up in his tale, as the picture of a mischievous little boy sneaking away from his teacher emerged, Kacie was scarcely aware of the jet's picking up speed. "How old were you?"

"Too young to know any better," he admitted wryly. The questioning look on her face drew a reluctant answer. "Nine."

"Go on," she prompted. "What happened after you lifted the lid?"

"What do you think?" he demanded.

Kacie's eyes lit with laughter. "A swarm came buzzing out to attack your unsuspecting person," she giggled, unable to suppress the vision of Jake hotfooting away from the irate insect squadron.

"Right on target," he agreed, grimacing at his unintentional pun. "Luckily, I escaped with only a couple of stings, but that was more than enough to give me a healthy respect for the little buzzers." He chuckled. "*And* a hatred for anything tasting of honey."

"I'll remember that."

Jake leaned across her slightly, staring out her window. "If you want to say good-bye, you'd better do it now," he suggested.

Startled, Kacie followed his gaze. They were airborne, she observed with shock. Atlanta lay below, an ever diminishing cluster of buildings. "That was quick." She gazed at Jake, gratitude in her eyes. "Thank you." For a moment she forgot all her resolutions, her determination to remain aloof. Once again Jake had scaled her defenses.

He returned her look, his eyes dark velvet shadows in his rugged face. "If you look at me like that, Irish, I might just forget my good intentions," he murmured.

Kacie blinked. Good intentions? "What good intentions?" she asked suspiciously. Warning bells clanged again in her mind.

"To give you time." He watched closely as his words penetrated.

"Time?" she echoed. She stirred slightly in her seat, becoming more aware with each passing second of how alone they were.

"Yes," he nodded, physically withdrawing and leaning back in his own place. "Why don't we get out of these harnesses?" He deftly put his suggestion into action and stood up. He waited long enough to see that she wasn't having any trouble with her belt, and then he headed for the bar.

Kacie followed slowly.

With his back to her, she had an opportunity to study him. This morning he wore a sable-colored suit, almost the exact shade of his hair. Obviously tailor-made for his muscular physique, it fit without a line or crease anywhere. The pale yellow shirt and the brown-and-gold silk tie were something of a shock. Kacie was accustomed to seeing him in the more conservative white shirt and dark tie.

"What will you have: juice, coffee, or something stronger?" he asked after surveying the contents of the refrigerator.

"Orange juice if you have it," she decided. She crossed to his side, realizing belatedly that she hadn't offered to help. "May I do anything?"

Jake glanced down at her, a devilish gleam in his eyes. "Well . . ." he drawled before plugging in the percolator.

"With the coffee," she qualified hurriedly.

He grinned, "What else?"

She picked up the chilled glass of fruit juice and retreated to the sofa. Damn the man, she fumed in dismay. She took a cooling sip of her drink, then another. Maybe she should leave Weston Technology after all.

"It isn't good to down icy liquids that way," he warned, coming across to join her, a steaming mug of coffee in his hand.

"Why not?" She knew she shouldn't snap at a simple remark like that, but she was wearying of this big cat-little mouse game he was playing.

"It'll give you a headache."

She glared at him. "I already have one." Her expression left no doubt as to who was the cause.

"My, my." He lowered his large frame onto the couch beside her. "Would an aspirin help?" he queried with apparent concern.

"No, but a new job might," she snapped, finally goaded past endurance. She knew she was overreacting, but she was powerless to stop herself. Her silent struggle to resist his allure augmented Jake's uncanny ability to ignite her temper with just a look or a word. No amount of resolve on her part seemed to restrain her inclination to rise to his baiting.

Suddenly the teasing light was gone from his eyes. His expression turned serious. "You wouldn't."

"How can you be sure?" she challenged, instinctively reacting to the certainty in his voice.

"Because you're no quitter. You may cling to that shell of yours a bit too much for my liking, but you're no coward," he avowed with a touch of surprise that she should need to ask.

"Escaping harassment couldn't possibly be termed quitting," she replied.

"Harassment!" He gave a snort of disbelief. "You can do better than that."

With careful precision she placed her empty glass on the table at her elbow. "What would you call it?"

"Any number of things. Interest. Curiosity. A desire to unearth the passion behind that wall you've built around yourself," he countered with blunt honesty. His gaze locked on her face, impaling her thoughts, probing her mind.

Caught in the intent midnight stare, Kacie read the truth. Whatever he wanted, it wasn't a one-night stand. She should have been reassured, but she wasn't. If anything, she was more worried than ever. To her knowledge Jake had attained every goal he'd ever set for himself. Knowing she was now his quarry increased her wariness.

"Why me?" she asked, her need to know too great to be denied.

Jake's eyes slowly traced her features. "Because you intrigue me with that neat nun's attitude hiding a razor-sharp brain, and with that madonnalike poise cloaking such volatile emotions."

"So, out of a whim you poke, prod, and provoke me to see my reactions. Is that it?" she demanded incredulously. This was even worse than she thought. To him she was little more than a curious mystery he wanted to solve.

He shook his head. "You really ought to watch your expression when you get mad, Irish," he chided. "And to answer the question you probably won't ask, I'm not toying with you, as the saying goes."

Kacie waited suspiciously for him to go on. It took a few seconds for her to realize that that was all he was going to say. Frustrated at what he had left unspoken, she stared helplessly at his bland expression. Blast his hide! He had done it again. She couldn't just ask if he intended to seduce her. Or could she? She eyed him consideringly.

"I wouldn't," he warned with a definitely knowing gleam.

For one mad moment she debated ignoring his advice, but something about the expectant quality of him suggested she wouldn't like the answer she got.

"I have some papers to take care of," he commented in a return to his more impersonal manner. Neither by look nor action did he indicate his victory over her in their short skirmish. "There are some magazines in the cabinet there." He gestured to the table beside her.

Gladly taking the hint, Kacie chose a popular business publication and immersed herself in it, hoping to blot out their last exchange. From time to time she studied Jake through lowered lashes as he worked. For a large man, he was oddly graceful. Each movement, each action, was precise and efficient. There was a lot to admire in him . . . if only he didn't aggravate her temper so often. This trip was likely to be even more trying than she'd expected, she acknowledged privately. Already she could feel herself succumbing to the lure of Jake's inexplicable appeal. Where was her resolve now?

"That's it." Jake glanced up from signing the last page of a fairly thick sheaf of papers. He checked his watch. "We should be catching a glimpse of Chicago soon," he observed, rising to his feet.

"Already?" Kacie commented, startled at how quickly the time had passed.

A muted *ping* of the seat-belt warning sounded.

"Right on time." He gestured toward the captain's chairs again. "Thanks for putting the glass and the coffee things away," he said as he took his place beside her.

Kacie nodded before turning to gaze out the window. Much as she preferred having her feet on terra firma, she wasn't about to forego her first look at Chicago. Plus, it provided the distraction she so desperately needed in the face of Jake's overwhelming masculinity so close by.

"That's Lake Michigan," Jake murmured near her ear.

Resolutely ignoring the frissons of pleasure rippling through her, Kacie focused her attention on the dark blue thumblike shape. "What's that?" she asked, her eyes on a hazy cloud at the tip of the lake. "Are those flames I see?"

"I'm afraid so. Those are the steel mills at Gary, Indiana." Jake directed her attention to the large cluster of buildings along the water's edge. "There's Chicago."

Kacie gasped as the plane descended. She could make out the huge structure she recognized from pictures as the Sears Tower, the world's tallest building.

"It looks like the granddaddy of them all," she observed on a note of whimsy.

Jake chuckled. "Well, it is. It has 109 stories, takes up a full city block, houses 16,000-plus employees, and has a power capacity equal to Rockford, the second-largest city in Illinois," he elaborated in a bad mimicry of a tour guide.

She couldn't resist testing how far his knowledge extended. Turning her head just enough to get a glimpse of his expression, she challenged him. "Is there more?"

The devil was back in his eyes as he took up her dare. "See that building over there?" He pointed to a shorter, although sill impressive, building. "That's the John Hancock Center—not that the locals call it anything but 'Big John.' It's the world's largest combined office-and-apartment building. It reaches 1,100 feet above ground level—"

"Okay, okay, I surrender." Kacie admitted defeat with a laugh. "I thought you were sealing a merger when you were here last, not sightseeing."

He shrugged. "Most of the time I was. But when I did escape the board room, Abbey was kind enough to show me around."

Kacie felt a momentary twinge of jealousy. The slight bump of the wheels touching the runway jerked Kacie out of her thoughts. She looked out the window in surprise before turning to Jake.

"You should patent that pre-takeoff and pre-landing chatter of yours," she advised lightly, although her eyes reflected her gratitude once again. "I forgot to be worried." She knew as soon as the words left her mouth that she shouldn't have given Jake such an opening. He didn't disappoint her.

"I keep telling you to trust yourself more..."—he paused—"...and while you're at it, me."

At a loss for a suitable reply, she stared helplessly at him. Fortunately the plane rolled to a stop, signaling the end of their flight. Between the disembarking process and collecting their luggage at the smaller private aircraft terminal, she was spared any further need for comment.

There was a limousine complete with a uniformed chauffeur waiting at the gate. In a matter of minutes she found herself in the roomy back seat, with Jake again at her side. Here they were even more intimately isolated than they'd been on the plane. Kacie's nerves tightened accordingly. She forced her mind to concentrate on her resolution, and she was pleased to feel some measure of poise flow back.

Curiosity and a need to concentrate on anything but the man next to her riveted her gaze to the scenery. The driver swung into the line of traffic on the Kennedy Expressway, heading for the downtown area. Kacie glanced toward O'Hare's huge main terminal buildings.

An involuntary gasp escaped her. "It's even bigger than Atlanta I," she exclaimed.

Jake nodded. "Look up in front," he directed quickly.

Obediently Kacie looked through the glass partition to the bridge ahead just in time to see a giant airplane wing swing out over the ribbon of traffic passing through the tunnel directly below.

"Good grief, what's that doing there?"

Jake chuckled, visibly amused at her open-mouthed surprise. "It's what is known as man's creative genius." The questioning arch of her dark brow prompted another grin. "They wanted to put a highway here as well as a taxiway for jets. So, true to Chicago's spirit, they did both. That underpass ahead runs beneath the airplane taxiway for this part of the field. So the expressway has its needs met by virtue of this tunnel, and the jumbo jets have their way because of the overpass."

"A compromise, in other words," she suggested.

"Right," he agreed. "However, it's a bit of a shock when you first look up and see the underside of a huge wing passing a few feet over your car."

"I agree," she said with feeling, suspiciously eyeing the jumbo jet currently inching along the raised ribbon of concrete.

"Don't look so worried," Jake chided, a smile tugging at his lips. "I promise if the plane comes through the roof," he began soothingly, "you won't know a thing about it."

For a moment it was a toss-up between giving him a very unladylike poke in the ribs, or releasing the laughter aching for expression. She began to chuckle, her sense of humor winning the day . . . *and* a look of unbelievable warmth, which threatened to turn her bones to melting honey.

5

KACIE INSPECTED HER small suite with satisfaction. Jake had been more than generous with her accommodations. The Drake was a stately hotel with a panoramic view of Lake Michigan, and it was very close to Jake's own apartment on North Lakeshore Drive.

She glanced at her watch. She had less than an hour to unpack and freshen up before Jake returned to collect her for lunch. A fleeting wish for something more attractive than her brown suit surfaced and was reluctantly banished. She didn't want Jake thinking she was dressing for him. That's all she needed after her abortive attempts to keep some distance between them.

Jake's knock sounded promptly at the specified hour, scant seconds after Kacie had completed a final combing of her hair.

She opened the door and stepped back, silently inviting him to enter.

"Good. You're ready," he remarked with a small nod. "Have you got your key?"

Recognizing the return of Jake the boss in his voice, she dangled the small brass object in the air without comment.

"Where are we going?" she asked after she had locked her door.

"There's an excellent restaurant nearby that specializes in seafood. I try to dine there whenever I get the chance," he explained as they stepped into the elevator.

"Fantastic," Kacie enthused. "I hope they have pompano."

Jake glanced at her curiously. "Don't tell me you're a seafood nut, too?"

She grinned, her eyes sparkling. "Mmm . . . addicted. Jumbo shrimp steamed in beer, trout Amandine, lobster Newburg . . ."

Jake chuckled. "Enough," he commanded. "I'm starving as it is."

Kacie smiled unrepentantly, enjoying the glow of pleasure she felt at Jake's response to her teasing. She wondered whether she was wise to take even this small initiative in their relationship, yet she couldn't resist the temptation. She was honest enough to admit that she was just a little piqued at how easily he could adopt his boss-type attitude.

The restaurant was everything Kacie could have hoped for, from its authentic decor to the antiques artfully arranged about the dining room. She surveyed the menu she held before glancing across the table to find Jake involved in a similar occupation.

Knowing she was momentarily safe from his perceptive gaze, she allowed her senses free rein to study the man across from her. In spite of herself, she couldn't stifle the allure he held for her. Even now—dressed in a conservative business suit, hunched over a lunch menu in a public place in broad daylight—he had the power to conjure up the memory of his last kiss...his last touch. Her eyes softened at the vision her mind was creating. For a traitorous moment she savored the warmth spreading through her. Jake snapped his menu closed, breaking the spell that held her captive. With a blink Kacie emerged from her trance and quickly smoothed her expression to one of polite interest. She was some kind of actress, she congratulated herself when Jake appeared not to notice her lapse. She breathed a mental sigh of relief when he began to speak.

"Have you decided what you'd like?" he asked.

"I thought New England clam chowder to start, then the steamed-shrimp basket," she answered, pleased her voice betrayed none of her turmoil.

Jake raised an eyebrow. "No pompano?"

She shook her head. "I couldn't resist the call of those shrimp."

"Then we'll make it two orders."

Like a genie out of a bottle, the waiter was beside them, pencil poised.

"You must come here often," Kacie commented when the man left after having voiced his respectful approval of their selections. She eyed the retreating figure thoughtfully. Even in this restaurant, Jake managed to make his presence felt. Not only had the hostess shown deference, but so had the rest of the staff. She turned to study her companion and found that he was watching her.

"You have the oddest expression on your face," he murmured pensively. "Care to tell me what you're thinking?"

Kacie blinked in surprise, caught off guard by his perception. "How do you do it?" she questioned before she thought.

"I'm afraid you're going to have to elaborate a bit," he replied dryly.

She gestured vaguely with one slim hand. "You know what I mean. Practically everyone around you bows to your slightest whim." She watched his eyes narrow at her bald pronouncement.

"That bothers you?" he asked, sounding annoyed.

She shook her head, instantly regretting her honesty. Jake looked anything but pleased at what she had intended as a compliment. "I didn't mean it that way," she explained, trying to erase the irritation she saw on his face.

"Oh?" He quirked one dark brow expressively.

Blast him! He had the most damnable habit of twisting her words, Kacie fumed silently. One two-lettered word made her feel as though she were accusing him of a major crime. "You know what I'm saying," she snapped, her own temper simmering.

Jake picked up his wine glass with cool deliberation and surveyed the clear white vintage before taking a sip. "For a hotshot computer specialist, you can sometimes be obscure," he observed as he replaced his drink on the table. He glanced up, neatly snagging her gaze. "You still haven't answered my question." He paused, his silence a demand for her response. "Does it bother *you?*"

Kacie noted the emphasis on his last word. Her eyes widened in comprehension. Somehow her answer mattered to him. But why? What difference could it possibly make to him how she viewed him?

"In a way," she admitted finally.

Jake's stare was intent, probing. "In what way?"

"Good grief, Jake," she laughed nervously, wishing she could think of some way to change the subject. Unfortunately, her usually quick mind was completely blank. "I only meant you are very successful...powerful even...People recognize it and react accordingly."

"Your chowder."

Kacie breathed her relief at the waiter's interruption, drawing a twisted smile from her companion.

Apparently deciding he wasn't going to get any more of an answer, Jake changed the subject. "There's been a change in plans."

"Oh?" she questioned, copying not only his pet response but also the intonation he gave it.

Jake registered her imitation but made no comment, although his eyes clearly expressed his opinion of her temerity.

"I have to meet with Mark this afternoon."

"That's all right. I can easily get a taxi and go on. It will give me a good chance to get acquainted..." Her voice trailed away as he shook his head.

"No. It would be better to wait until morning, when I can be there to introduce you," he stated uncompromisingly.

"A phone call could do that," she argued.

"No."

Kacie put down her spoon, eyeing Jake's calm face. "Why not?" she demanded in what she hoped was a reasonable manner. Surely Jake didn't believe her incapable of such a simple task as meeting the Chicago staff. She had been so certain he accepted her ability.

His jaw clenched, deepening the lines about his mouth. Kacie could feel the powerful hold he was exerting over his anger at her continued questioning of his authority. She was amazed at her own tenaciousness. What was wrong with her that she felt she must buck every decision he made? As her boss, he was well within his rights to command her time during business hours. She opened her lips to deliver the apology she knew he deserved, but his cold voice stilled her words.

"May I remind you, you work for me."

She nodded, warned by the fire in his eyes that it would be wise to agree meekly.

"I'm sure you can find something to do with yourself until dinner tonight. See the sights or whatever."

"I will," Kacie murmured sweetly as the waiter returned with their main course.

Jake waited until the man departed before continuing. "Just one thing." He paused until Kacie met his eyes. "Don't go anywhere without checking with the hotel. There are places here that are unsafe even in broad daylight. It's not like Atlanta, where you know what trouble areas to avoid.

Kacie's expression must have betrayed her skepticism.

"I mean it, Kacie," Jake warned impatiently. "Ask at the desk if you don't believe me." Picking up a luscious pink shrimp, he peeled the shell off with one deft flick of his fingers. Unwillingly mesmerized, Kacie watched him lift the morsel to his lips, open them, and pop the shrimp into his mouth.

She had seen Jake in many moods: cajoling, teasing, gentle, even angry, but never had she seen him so thoroughly provoked.

"Jake, I'm—" she began, hating the tension enveloping them.

"Leave it," he interrupted shortly. "Just eat your lunch."

She continued to stare at him for a few seconds, mentally willing him to lift his head. When he continued to ignore her, focusing instead on his meal, she, too, started to eat. After the mess she had made so far, she didn't have the nerve to say anything else—even if it was an apology.

Lunch was a strained affair that seemed to drag on for hours, at least from Kacie's point of view. Jake was coldly polite, to the edge of formality. She found it increasingly difficult to keep her temper. She had shifted from feeling apologetic to being annoyed at his attitude. By the time she watched him stride toward the main entrance of the hotel, leaving her standing alone in the busy lobby, she was blessing Abbey's uncle for requiring Jake's presence this afternoon.

With an inward grimace of disgust at how far she had allowed herself to be influenced by the maddening male, she turned and made her way to the reception desk.

"May I help you?"

Kacie forced herself to smile at the pretty blond desk clerk. "I thought I'd do some shopping, but since I've never been here before, I don't know where to go."

"For clothes or gifts?"

Kacie glanced down at her brown suit, then back at the girl. She grinned ruefully. "Definitely the first."

There was a decided twinkle in the green eyes of the younger women. "State Street and the Loop are good places to begin. Most of the big department stores are there," she offered. "And if you really want something special, try Michigan Avenue's Magnificent Mile."

"I only have an afternoon," Kacie warned, her mind ticking off the list of possibilities.

"Don't worry, they're all in this general area. Do you have a car?"

Kacie shook her head.

"Then a taxi would be your best bet, since you don't know your way around."

Kacie thanked her youthful adviser and headed for the doors. Once outside she was assailed by a brisk breeze, almost as though the lusty city sought to imprint its nickname on each person within its hold. A bright yellow cab was waiting at the curb, as though ordered especially for her. Kacie concluded it was a good omen for her excursion. Deciding the Magnificent Mile had a name too intriguing to be missed, she asked the driver to make it their first stop.

Water Tower Place, a huge conglomerate of a shopping center, was the anchor for the "Mile," with a theater, restaurants, a hotel, Marshall Field & Co., and Lord & Taylor among its tenants. According to her talkative cabbie, the address also boasted branches of prestigious emporia such as Bonwit Teller, Saks, Gucci, I. Magnin Co. and Tiffany & Co.

Once inside, Kacie was astounded at the beauty of the large mall. Vividly blooming flowers bordered the many lush trees and plants dotted around the various levels and lining the several escalators. It was pleasantly cool, with the mingled scents of fine goods and expensive colognes creating that special aura of éliteness. Although Kacie was accustomed to Atlanta's exclusive areas, she found that Water Tower Place more than lived up to its address. It would have been a treat simply to browse, even if she hadn't had a long shopping list to fill.

Having decided to shed her colorless image like a butterfly emerging from its cocoon, Kacie reveled in the hues, textures, and styles of the glittering array of fashions displayed in each store. Whatever scruples she had about her chrysalis she buried with the late Miss Daniels.

By the time she returned to her hotel suite, she was laden with a small mountain of packages, each sporting a distinguished label. Finding one chair that wasn't bearing its share of the load, she sat down with a sigh and kicked off her shoes, wriggling her aching toes. She was exhausted. Shopping was definitely not an easy chore, she mused as she relaxed against the soft cushions of her seat.

With a grin she surveyed the results of her raid on the Chicago merchants. She wished Jan could see her now. Her outspoken friend probably would have fainted dead away at her sudden change of heart. Except for horses, new fashions were Jan's favorite topics of conversation.

"Enough of that," Kacie said to herself when she glanced at her watch. She didn't have much time to get ready for dinner.

It took some searching to locate the dress and matching lingerie she had chosen for the evening. She decided to ask a hotel maid to unpack the rest after she'd left. From her handbag she extracted a small box and headed for the bathroom. She had been looking forward to this moment since mid-afternoon.

"Fill regular size tub with warm water and add one-half cup of dry milk crystals," she read aloud from the handwritten instructions she held. She eyed the pink tub dubiously, then stared back at the box of ordinary powdered milk. "She can't be serious," she mumbled, reaching over to plug the drain and turn on the taps.

She had heard about milk baths before, but this was the first time she had ever thought to try one. If it hadn't been for the saleswoman in Saks, she wouldn't be emptying the handful she guessed to be equal to half a cup into the tub. Remembering the lady's exquisite complexion, Kacie decided she had nothing to lose.

Within seconds of sliding into the cloudy white liquid, she knew the woman hadn't exaggerated. Already her skin felt more silky than she had believed possible. Even the aches were leaving her tired body. She couldn't resist luxuriating in the rich froth until the cooling temperature of the water and the creeping hands of the clock forced her to rinse off and reach for a fluffy towel.

An hour later found her seated and watching the time slip away. Jake was late. She felt like a teenager on her first date, nervous and shy about Jake's reaction. It had seemed such a simple, foolproof plan to change her image that Kacie wanted to laugh aloud at her naiveté. For in her haste to eliminate one battleground from the strange war between her and Jake, she had stumbled into a brand new mine field. By altering her appearance, she had not only shown Jake just how much his words had touched her, she had also made herself over into the kind of woman he was probably accustomed to dating. And, knowing him, she was certain he would take the new her as a sign of victory.

What was worst of all, however, was that she, herself, wasn't honestly certain about her motives any longer. It wasn't that she wanted him to . . . She let the sentence die, unwilling to put a name to her need for Jake's approval. In the light of day it was easy enough to say she wanted to win at least one skirmish in this peculiar battle. At night . . . well . . .

Kacie glanced at the door for the tenth time in as many minutes, then started when the phone at her elbow shrilled.

"Kacie, I'm not going to be able to have dinner with you," Jake announced without even the courtesy of a greeting.

Unable to believe her ears, she was silent.

"Are you there?" Impatience edged the question, stirring Kacie's temper as well as her tongue.

"Yes," she replied briefly, gazing down at the beautiful dress she had bought specifically for this evening.

"I haven't got much time. Call down to room service and have them send something up for tonight, okay? I'll pick you up in the morning at about eight."

She responded automatically, even while her mind was seething with various descriptive epithets for his cavalier treatment of her.

"Okay."

Her brief agreement signaled the end of their exchange as the dial tone in her ear indicated he had hung up.

"Damn your Yankee hide, Jake Weston! Of all the inconsiderate . . . aggravating . . ." She flung the receiver into its resting place with a loud bang, then brutally kicked off her expensive high-heeled silver shoes. "I should have known better than to try to outfox him," she muttered, irately sending her matching handbag sailing in the general direction of her evening slippers. Barefoot, she stalked into her bedroom, her hands feeling for and finding her dress zipper.

With one angry yank the pink-and-lavender-print creation floated to the carpet, where she stepped out of its gossamer folds. "The least he could have done was apologize . . . maybe even explain," she protested to the empty room. Whirling around, she stared at the colored pool of soft fabric a few feet away. As quickly as it had flared, her temper died. Slowly, step by step, she approached the discarded gown. As she bent over to pick it up, tiny drops of water fell onto her outstretched hands. When she straightened and caught her reflection in the vanity mirror, the subdued lighting of the bedside lamp glistened on the silver streams streaking her cheeks like fragile moonbeams from sapphire pools of self-revelation. She, a woman of logic and control, had been so blind she had not known her own heart. She glanced at the symbol of her plea for the giant's approval.

Approval . . . ha! Such a tame word for what she really wanted. Passion! Desire! *Love!* The last word emblazoned itself across her mind, reaching to its farthest recesses. She felt the shock of it drive the color from her face as she sank weakly to the bed and stared out the window. Chicago in all its night-shrouded beauty did not exist. She saw nothing . . . felt everything.

She lay down curled on her side on top of the bedspread, her dress still clutched in one hand. Hypnotized by lights of buildings nearby, she lay silently until her lashes finally fluttered shut, wiping out her realizations and bringing relief to her battered emotions.

Dawn streaked Kacie's bed with a blush of pink as her eyelids flickered once, then opened fully. For a long moment she remained motionless, her memories of the night before pouring back and dispelling the lingering mists of sleep. But there was a difference. She knew it immediately. It was as if some magical being had touched her as she slumbered. The confusion, the bewilderment, and the nervousness she had known were gone. In their place was acceptance and a calm sense of rightness. She was whole again and in control. The knowledge brought a smile to her lips and a surge of energy that needed a place to go.

She rolled over to check the time. Laughter bubbled up at the thought of the two hours she had to herself before she saw Jake. She sat up, noticing her crumpled dress on the floor beside the bed.

"To the pressers with you, my friend," she commanded gaily before reaching for the phone to order breakfast. Suddenly she was ravenous.

Her state of euphoria lasted through her breakfast of eggs Benedict and her preparations for work. Unlike the night before, there was no nervousness in her wait for Jake. Somehow, knowing that she loved him had given her an impregnable armor. She was free of the past and secure in the present. The future was immaterial. She expected nothing different from Jake just because she had changed. But since she recognized her love for him, she felt no fear of either the emotion or the man who inspired it. She would take each minute, each hour, each day as it came. What Jake felt, she had no idea. In fact, in some strange way, it didn't matter . . . for now, at least. It was enough to finally recognize her own emotions. She knew she had to be very careful not to betray herself, but even that didn't have the power to daunt her in her present mood. It was such a relief to understand the conflict that had torn her apart for so long.

In the mirror she saw that her face, her whole attitude, reflected her altered thinking. She wondered if Jake would notice. It was a measure of her new-found serenity that she was able to open the door at his brisk knock without a trace of hesitation.

"Hi," she greeted him good-naturedly. She ran her

eyes over his massive form, noting the lines of weariness etching his rugged features. His hair was darker than usual from the dampness of his morning shower. A desire to wipe away the marks of strain from his powerful frame rose within her. She ached to comfort him, to soothe him with her touch and the softness of her body. Only hours ago such feelings would have frightened her into retreating, but not now.

"You look tired," she observed sweetly, stepping back so he could enter. "Would you like some coffee? I ordered an extra cup just in case."

Jake eyed her narrowly, puzzlement flickering briefly across his face. "You obviously slept well last night," he observed, taking a seat at her gesture toward the sofa.

She nodded. She brought his coffee over and put it on the low table in front of the couch. "Must be that early night I had," she murmured without rancor.

There was a slight tinge of red along Jake's cheekbones as he winced at her comment. "I know I owe you an apology," he admitted in a tone that showed how seldom he did such a thing. He picked up his cup and took a sip.

Kacie grinned, her ego getting a definite boost at his discomfiture. For once she wasn't the one on the receiving end.

"You don't need to rub it in," he grumbled, accurately reading her expression. He downed the rest of his coffee in one gulp. "I bet the other wives weren't so—"

Kacie giggled—she couldn't help it. He looked like a little boy caught with his hand in the cookie jar. "Other wives?" she queried in mock innocence.

Jake eyed her balefully. "Damn it, you know what I mean." He shot an impatient look at his wristwatch. "Can we continue this post-mortem on the way?"

She was tempted to sit there and watch her usually cool tormentor get out of the corner he had backed himself into, but good sense won the day. The lion might be a little off balance now that he was tired, but she knew darned well it was at best a temporary condition. But, oh, it was so good to know she wasn't the only one capable of awkwardness.

Shrugging casually, she rose and picked up her handbag. Jake was silent on the way to his car. Kacie darted quick sidelong peeks, trying to gauge his mood. She could feel the speculation in his eyes as he glanced her way. She knew he sensed the change in her and was puzzled by it. Probably his razor-sharp mind was already at work trying to solve the mystery of her sudden poise.

She pretended to study the passing buildings as Jake eased into the mainstream of traffic. In reality she was enjoying her new sense of security—reveling in it, actually, she acknowledged with inner amusement.

"Mark is having a get-together in a few days," Jake announced, braking at a stoplight. He darted a quick look in her direction before moving forward again. "Most of the larger ex-stockholders will be there."

"Business or pleasure?" she asked, wondering at his odd inflection.

"A little of both, I imagine," he replied unhelpfully before adding the clincher. "I'll leave you to decide."

She raised an eyebrow at the obvious statement of a command attendance. "What day?" she refused to argue with his method of invitation as she would have in the past.

Jake quickly glanced her way, his eyes glimmering with amusement. "Has Irish taken the morning off?" he asked, ignoring her question.

Kacie suppressed the childish urge to poke her tongue out at him. "She's gone for good," she murmured self-righteously.

"That's too bad," he replied in a sorrowful tone. "I really liked that woman."

"Isn't that just too—" she started to say.

"I'll bet I can get her back," he challenged, swinging smoothly into a multistoried parking garage.

She stared at him, resenting the assurance in his tone but having no intention of reacting as he obviously wanted. "Good luck," she countered sweetly.

Surprised, Jake shot her an intense look. She knew he was thinking that the woman at his side bore little resemblance to the Kacie he had come to know. For one thing, she was beautifully dressed in a royal blue suit and a paler blue silk blouse, which added depth to her eyes and highlights to her hair. No longer confined to that long switch tied at the back of her neck, her hair was styled in a simple chignon, which accentuated the fine bones of her face. Her mirror had attested that she looked cool, elegant, and poised.

"Something wrong?" Her softly voiced question visibly startled Jake out of his trance.

"I'm not sure yet," he answered quietly, seemingly unconscious of speaking his thoughts aloud.

Kacie hid a smile as he slid out of his seat. It was going to be a beautiful day! In fact, gorgeous, she decided, slipping out of her own side.

Jake gestured toward the far wall and the elevators.

"I'm not sure of the time of Mark's get-together. I'll have to let you know." Without a blink he returned to their interrupted conversation. "It should be interesting if everyone from last night can make it."

"Last night?"

The elevator doors glided shut. "Mark's idea. He thought the ladies deserved a treat for the ruined plans they suffered because of our meeting."

"Meeting?" Blast! She sounded like an echoing parrot. The telltale twitch of Jake's lips confirmed that he had similar thoughts. Well, what did he expect if he was going to hand out his explanations piecemeal, she rationalized rebelliously.

"Oh, didn't I tell you?"

You know you haven't said one word, my dear Mr. Weston, she mentally assured him grimly, *but I'm not about to lose my temper and tell you so.*

"No," she replied calmly, stepping out when the elevator reached their floor.

"We had a small stock problem connected with the merger that we had to iron out." He nodded pleasantly to the pretty blond receptionist who greeted him as he ushered Kacie past the office lobby. "We go this way," he directed, a large hand pressed against the middle of her back, urging her forward. "I'll take you through to the computer lab and introduce you to John Lockhart. He already knows you're coming." He leaned forward to open a door to another corridor, which was starkly different from the colorful one they had just left.

Here the walls were an icy blue, the carpet underfoot a multitoned indigo. The combination was cool and restful, unlike the vibrant yellows and tangerines of the reception area and the business section. Kacie instantly felt at home, her mind already shifting to the problems she was likely to encounter shortly.

"It smells as though it's just been painted."

"It has. I don't like nondescript green walls."

Kacie glanced at him, thinking how typical his statement was of his whole attitude. What he didn't approve of he changed. No compromise, no discussion—just action.

"No comment?"

"I can't stand them either," she admitted. "This is much better." She waved an expressive hand.

"At least we agree on something," he murmured quietly as he pushed open the door.

Kacie glanced around, finding the room little different from the one she worked in at the Atlanta office. That was a relief, she decided with an inaudible sigh.

To her right, about six feet from the wall, stood the main memory of the system. Next to it stood two disc-drive units with their distinctive bronze-tone acrylic cases perched atop the large square cabinets. Kacie's knowledgeable eye had already determined the model as the same she was accustomed to.

She and Jake stepped onto the slight incline that led to the raised floor above the cables of the complex machines. She felt the familiar vibration of the temperature-controlled air passing through the ducts under her feet. While the advent of the printed circuit board had made the equipment less sensitive, a certain temperature range still had to be maintained.

The room was deserted except for one slender brown-haired man, who rose from his console at their entrance.

"Hello, John," Jake greeted him. "This is Kacie Daniels. Kacie, John Lockhart."

Kacie smiled, instantly warming to the owner of the twinkling hazel eyes that gazed admiringly at her.

* * *

"So you're the wonder lady," John commented with a welcoming grin.

She gave a dismissive shrug, faintly embarrassed by his obvious approval. She wasn't accustomed to such immediate acceptance.

"I had a chance to go over your brain child last night," he went on. "It's quite impressive.

"Not mine," Kacie denied, slanting a glance at Jake's bland expression. "It was a joint effort." She couldn't tell whether or not he was pleased by her admission. Not that it mattered, because she had no intention of taking credit for someone else's work anyway.

John showed confusion, looking to his boss for clarification. He didn't get it. If anything, Jake's face was even more insrutable.

"I'll leave you two to get on with it," he directed. "I have a meeting shortly." Without so much as a goodbye, he headed for the door, leaving Kacie facing her co-worker.

"That's Jake," John remarked in the slightly awkward silence between them. He chuckled, revealing even white teeth. "I never knew what energy was until I met him." Admiration for the older man came through clearly.

"He does have a knack for getting quite a bit done in a very short time," she agreed . . . even if his manners falter periodically, she added silently. "Where may I put my bag?"

"Here." John opened an empty desk drawer. "There's an extra coat in the closet over there. We don't have to wear them, but I find they help keep out the chill."

Nodding, Kacie took out a chalk-white full-length jacket, slipped it over her suit, and then slid her glasses onto her nose.

"That's more like it," John teased, eyeing her businesslike garb.

"More like a computer lady, you mean," she shot back, not in the least offended by his banter. It was impossible not to respond to John's good humor. His attitude was relaxing, and she was grateful. Here at least she didn't have to concern herself with the complexities of a man like Jake.

"Okay, let's get started."

Kacie put all outside thoughts aside as she concentrated on the job at hand. There was a great deal of work involved in reprogramming a system of this size. Not only did the new procedures need to be compatible with the existing ones, but she also had to see to the hook-up on the loop with Atlanta and New York. Kacie positioned herself in front of the master console and began the step-by-step process of identifying herself and 'talking' to the computer. Obligingly, the dark gray screen responded with a stream of tiny electronic green letters and symbols. The initial stages went through beautifully. Near lunchtime, though, a definite problem developed to halt their progress.

"That's the third time it's thrown it back at us," John observed unnecessarily. His light brows were drawn together in a frown as he scanned the printout sheets in his hand. "I don't see the hang-up."

"May I?" Kacie took the green-and-white gridded papers and spread them carefully over the desk. For a long moment she studied the mechanized language. "Let's try eliminating this stage and see what happens," she suggested finally.

John peered over her shoulder. "Could do." He nodded thoughtfully. "It might work." He smiled at her, his

eyes nearly on a level with her own. "It can't hurt, anyway. Do you want to do it now or wait until after lunch?"

Kacie glanced at her watch. "First tell me how good
the food is, then I'll answer your question," she teased.

"Super, actually."

"Then we'll eat first."

John chuckled. "A lady after my own heart."

"Oh no, I'm not," she laughed, slipping out of her
coat and retrieving her handbag.

"Okay," he shrugged, not in the least abashed. "You
can't blame a guy for—"

"Trying," she finished for him. "I know, but not in
my direction." She followed him as he led the way to
the company cafeteria.

"You sound positive." He slanted her a curious look.
"Are you Jake's girl?"

Startled, she paused outside the swinging doors of the
dining room. "Jake?" she echoed. "Not a chance."

She pushed open the right panel and entered. The
warm, sunny colors of the lobby were vividly reproduced
in the modern setting of the company eatery. The subdued
hum of many voices and the muted clatter of cutlery
pleasantly enveloped them. Kacie followed John down
the line, pushing her tray before her.

"There's an empty table over there," John directed
after paying their bill. "Okay with you?"

She nodded. She marveled at how much simpler it
was to make friends here than at home. A short time
ago, she probably would have chosen to eat out rather
than run the gauntlet of interested stares now following
their progress to the vacant table. And never would she
have felt this much at ease with a stranger, especially a
male. Yet here she was in a city she had never visited,

laughing and chatting with a man she'd just met. True, there was no physical attraction on her part, but she did enjoy his presence. One point in his favor was that he didn't arouse her temper or her defenses. It was such a pleasure not to have to guard every word she uttered.

"You know, you really are a surprise."

Kacie glanced up from her plate, one eyebrow lifting in question.

"You're not at all what any of us expected." John chuckled, his hazel eyes conveying an amused apology. "I always thought I was a product of the times and more equality conscious. After seeing you, I've decided I'm not. I'm afraid I fell into the stereotype trap."

As little as a week ago, Kacie would have felt a slow boil of anger at John's confession. Now she experienced no need to jump to her own defense. She shrugged casually and smiled back. "Don't worry about it. I think I'm becoming immune to people's shock."

"Good. At least I won't need to spend a few days getting back onto your good side before asking you to have dinner with me," he stated with definite satisfaction.

Kacie hesitated for a moment. While she wasn't averse to John's friendly admiration, she preferred maintaining the status quo. She didn't want the complication of another man in her life. Jake was quite enough.

"No strings," John added, seeing her indecision. "In fact, I'll even offer to show you Chicago. An official unofficial tour guide, if you like."

She eyed him speculatively. If he meant what he said, he was the answer to her problem of what to do with her spare time. Normally, she wouldn't have even considered using anyone as a shield, but . . .

"You're sure?" she questioned at last.

"Seven o'clock tonight all right with you?" John asked in reply.

Feeling committed, Kacie nodded. For one second she wondered what Jake's reaction would be. Or if he would even have one.

6

THAT EVENING KACIE took her time primping for her date with John. The pink-and-lavender dress from her aborted date with Jake lay pressed and ready on the end of her bed. Recalling Jake's stunned reaction to her refusal to dine with him tonight brought a thoughtful frown to her face as she smoothed the silky material over her hips. She couldn't shake the feeling that he had really been disappointed. It was ridiculous for a man like him to react that way over something as trivial as a dinner engagement. The moment it reared its head, she squelched the memory of her own recent reaction to Jake's last-minute cancellation.

She turned to survey herself in the mirror, and liked what she saw. Gone was the nunlike Miss Daniels, and in her place was a colorful butterfly stranger she hardly recognized. If nothing else, Jake's forceful appearance in her life had made her shed her drab cocoon for all time. She enjoyed the new Kacie too much to want to revert to her drab other self. The feel of lush fabrics and the look of vivid colors appealed to her senses. She was young and very much alive, and she knew it. Never again would she use her work as an excuse for living.

She eyed the daring V neck of the bodice with approval. Last night she had worried whether it exposed too much. Tonight she had no such fears. She had seen much deeper plunges than hers in her recent amblings. She involuntarily wondered what Jake would say if he saw it.

Then her practical nature asserted itself. "He isn't likely to, remember? John not Jake, is taking you out," she reminded her image. *But it could have been Jake,* the stranger in the mirror replied.

"No way," Kacie denied emphatically. "He stood me up."

He had a good reason. Admit it, girl. You don't want to spend the evening with him because you're afraid he might find out your secret—he might discover that you love him.

Kacie glared at her accuser.

Face it, Kacie, you're still hiding in your safe little world. Oh, the gossamer wings are of brilliant hues, but Miss Daniels is still safe beneath all that vivid display.

For a long second she stared at her reflection, not really seeing it at all. She looked inward, reading the truth emblazoned in her mind. A sharp knock destroyed the moment of self-realization. Forcing a pleasant expression to her face, she went to open the door.

John's happy smile when she greeted him was reward enough for the effort she had made. Banishing all thoughts of Jake, she returned John's smile, determined not to spoil his evening.

"You're one gorgeous lady," John pronounced, guiding her to the elevator.

Responding to his good humor, Kacie found herself relaxing slightly. "You're not too bad yourself." She glanced with approval at the gray suit he wore. It was impossible to avoid comparing John with her giant. Now why had she labeled him thus, she wondered fleetingly. Jake was his own man—definitely no woman's. Dismayed at the way her thoughts were straying, she turned her attention back to her date, catching the tail end of his plans for the evening.

". . . Does that sound good to you?" John questioned in concern.

Unwilling to admit she hadn't heard a word he'd said, she nodded, praying she hadn't let herself in for something she loathed. John's choice proved to be as soothing as he was.

From the valet parking at the traditionally elegant Tremont Hotel to Cricket's attractive dining room, Kacie felt pampered on her first night on the town. Soft lighting glowed over crisp linen and gleaming silver as the staff moved about discreetly.

"Do you like quail?" John asked as the waiter appeared with the menu.

She nodded.

"Terrific. That's another thing we have in common."

Turning her attention to the menu in front of her, Kacie smiled without comment. The teasing light in John's eyes told her not to take him seriously. There was a short silence while they made up their minds. She laid down her list and told John her selection. She listened absently while he transmitted their orders.

"We'll start with escargots Bourguignon, then a brace of roast quail . . ."

Kacie glanced slowly around the room. There was someone staring at her, she could feel it. Her gaze slipped over a shadowy corner table, moved past for a split second before flying back as her mind assimilated Jake's broad-shouldered form. A small shudder went through her as she caught his steady ebony stare. He lifted his wine glass in recognition, his eyes never leaving hers. She tried to subdue the blush she felt rising at the way he was watching her. The quirk of his lips told her she hadn't succeeded.

Deliberately, she turned back to John's undemanding company. She wouldn't let Jake spoil her evening. She knew she should tell John about Jake's presence, but she didn't want to be forced to invite him to join them. Right now, all she really wanted to do was forget her large pursuer.

As dinner progressed, Kacie became increasingly tense. Time after time she had to force her attention to remain on her dinner partner and to deny the magnetic pull of Jake's waiting shadow. She hadn't looked around since the initial glance, but she knew he was still there . . . watching.

When John suggested they visit a popular nightclub for after-dinner dancing, Kacie jumped at the opportunity to escape Jake's presence. She should have known he wasn't the type of man to back off or to stay patiently in the background. John had no sooner called for the check than Kacie looked up to see Jake towering over their table. She didn't for a moment trust the genial smile creasing his rugged face, even though she returned it with one of her own. Up until now John hadn't been aware that his boss was in the room.

"Mr. Weston," he greeted the older man.

"John." Jake eyed the bill on the table. "Are you two leaving already?" he asked casually, although Kacie saw a determined gleam in his dark eyes.

"I promised Kacie I'd take her dancing," he explained. "Would you and your date . . ." John hesitated, obviously just realizing there wasn't anyone with Jake.

"I'm afraid my lady stood me up," Jake offered with a chuckle and a sidelong glance at Kacie's still figure. "I'm all alone. I hope the invitation is still open though?" One dark brow lifted in question.

"Of course," John agreed heartily as he rose to his feet.

Kacie stared into Jake's black eyes, reading the challenge there. Smiling when she really felt more like clouting her tormentor, she silently conceded. Flanked by the two men, she moved toward the elevators. John appeared totally unconcerned. In fact, Kacie decided privately, he was probably enjoying being singled out by a man of Jake's stature. While she . . . she felt outmaneuvered . . . again. Darn him!

"How's this?" John asked, pulling out a chair for Kacie. "It gives us a good view without our having to shout," he added, indicating the band tuning up on the slightly raised stage.

"This is fine." Kacie sank thankfully into the seat he held for her.

With an approving nod, Jake took the chair on her left side, leaving the third for John. Typically, the table was small—little more than a stand for a few drinks. Kacie knew it was going to be next to impossible not to bump elbows and knees periodically. Disturbed at the way Jake had so easily taken over her date as well as cramped her space, she withdrew as far as possible into her chair.

Then the evening began to take on an entirely different complexion. As irritated as she was at Jake, she couldn't control her own immediate response to his potent presence. Her senses were sparking to life, a slow warmth unfurling within her. And that involuntary reaction only served to make her more annoyed than ever—and more alarmingly conscious of his masculine allure.

Other than requesting a bourbon and soda, an unnerved Kacie allowed John to carry the burden of the conversation. Talk drifted to the subject of computers as they awaited their drinks. The musicians finished setting up and launched into a fast number that attracted a few brave souls onto the empty floor.

"Shall we, Kacie?"

She glanced up, seeing John's eager expression. With a smile and a murmured "Excuse me" to Jake, she got to her feet. She tossed her head like a high-mettled mare at Jake's open amusement over her quick acceptance. Served him right for butting in on her date, she thought rebelliously, following John to the cleared area in front of the stage.

Once there, Kacie abandoned the last of her inhibitions. She threw herself into the music, letting the pulsating beat surge through her. It felt so good to work out her frustrations and the tension caused by Jake's hovering shadow. She laughed aloud at the shock on John's face at her fluid interpretations. The silvery ripple of sound echoed the pure enjoyment she was experiencing. With only a moment's hesitation, John emulated her graceful movements. Both were breathless when the number ended.

Jake rose politely at their return, and somehow when

he sat down again, his chair was even closer to Kacie's. She felt a muscled thigh brush hers as they settled back, and she hastily rearranged her legs. Seething with resentment, she ached to tell Jake exactly what she thought of his high-handed methods. Yet another part of her pulsated with pleasure and delicious excitement over the trouble he had obviously taken to track her down. The woman in her responded strongly to his possessiveness.

"Am I crowding you?" Jake asked solicitously as he made a show of shifting his chair without really moving it.

Kacie could feel his amusement at her position as she politely murmured, "A bit, yes." What she ought to do was put an elegant little elbow into his side, she thought maliciously. The only thing stopping her from doing just that was not knowing how he would retaliate.

If John noticed her barely concealed discomfiture it didn't appear to bother him. Kacie almost choked on her drink when Jake tapped her lightly on her arm. She knew what was coming, and there wasn't one way she could think of to refuse.

"May I?" he asked, his eyes on John.

At John's generous "Of course," Kacie silently walked ahead of Jake toward the crowded dance floor, where the band had just begun a slow, sensuous number guaranteed to raise the lowest blood pressure. She shot Jake an annoyed glance as he swung her into his arms. Instead of the conventional dance position she expected, she found herself in an intimate embrace. Imprisoned against his massive body, she instinctively resisted, trying to free herself from his overwhelming masculinity. She opened her lips to protest his style, but he didn't give her the chance.

"I ought to beat you, Kacie Daniels," he remarked in a low rumble. "But since I see Irish has decided to come out of hiding, I'll just be thankful instead."

Kacie's mouth snapped shut as she realized how close she had come to playing into Jake's hands by losing her temper. Oh, how she would love to plant a heel in one of his nicely polished shoes, preferably where the leather was the thinnest. She stared at the knot of his tie, savoring the image of him hopping about on one foot.

"No comment?"

She shook her head.

"A pity," he drawled, pulling her closer into his arms. "Although on second thought, maybe I like this new side of your personality better. It certainly is softer—and much more pliable."

Kacie immediately stiffened, catching his reference to the way she melted into his arms. What a fool she was. How could she have betrayed herself so?

"Now don't go all defensive again," he chided as she stumbled against him. His arms tightened around her. His chuckle sounded at her temple. "I was hoping the war was over."

Kacie felt his hand move seductively beneath the long hair cascading down her back. She involuntarily shivered.

"Jake, stop it!" she commanded in a hoarse whisper.

"Why?" he asked softly, his breath stirring her hair. "I like the feel of you, especially the way you fit in my arms." His fingers glided lightly down her spine in a provocative caress.

Every nerve tingled, alive with sensation. "Jake, I mean it. I don't know why you invited yourself along, but—" She got no further.

"Don't you, Irish?" he shot back quickly. He was forced to stop dancing when she came to a complete halt in his arms.

"You can let go now," she murmured as the number ended. She wanted to escape as quickly as possible.

Jake dropped his arms with obvious reluctance and allowed her to precede him to their table.

Kacie saw the curiosity in John's gaze as she took her seat. She didn't miss the speculative look he divided between her and their boss. She held his glance with difficulty. No doubt he had seen her and Jake dancing—the way they were dancing—and had drawn his own conclusions.

When John stood up at the beginning of the next selection, Kacie accepted, although she wished she'd had the nerve to refuse. Even given the "no strings" aspect of their evening, it was stretching any man's good humor to ask him to sit idly by while another male took over his date. It didn't matter that the female in question was providing no encouragement at all—unless he counted her small lapse on the dance floor, she admitted fairly.

"John, I'm sorry," she began, hoping to forestall any questions. "I had no idea Jake would invite himself along."

"Didn't you?" he asked skeptically. She stiffened indignantly, but he ignored it. "I asked you this morning if I was poaching on Jake's territory. You said no."

She stared John in the eye, surprised at the emotion—anger, almost—reflected on his face. She resented being labeled anyone's territory. She tried a reasonable approach. "I know you're annoyed. I can't—"

John interrupted her. "Do you want me to leave? I can, you know."

Kacie was aghast. This whole evening was assuming

nightmarish proportions, and it was all Jake's fault. "Of course I don't want you to leave. Do you honestly think I planned this?"

For a moment she was sure he was going to say yes. Then she felt him relax slightly, saw his expression soften. "No, I guess not," he admitted slowly. He whirled her away from a clumsy couple before adding, "I wonder if Jake did?"

Kacie had the same thought, and as the evening progressed she became certain of it. For every dance she had with John, she also had one with Jake. While Jake did nothing more than repeat his unconventional dancing style, Kacie became increasingly edgy. When John finally suggested they call it a night, she agreed with alacrity.

She didn't count on Jake's offering to drive her back to the hotel. John's refusal was gallantly prompt, but it held no ground against Jake's reasonable response. Jake pointed out that John's apartment lay in the opposite direction of Kacie's hotel, while the Drake was on Jake's way home. Good sense on John's part not to argue in view of the boss's obvious determination tipped the scales in Jake's favor.

With little more than a hurried good-bye, Kacie found herself escorted to Jake's car and handed in. Retreating into offended silence, she studied the passing scenery with seeming all-consuming interest.

"Sulking?" Jake asked in an amused tone, flicking a quick glance at her averted profile.

"No," she answered shortly without turning her head.

"Liar," he chuckled softly in the darkness, a surprisingly intimate sound that stoked the fires of her frustration.

"Just drive the car, Jake. The sooner I'm at the hotel, the better," she muttered, clamping her teeth shut on her simmering temper. She . . . would . . . not . . . yell!

A low laugh mocked her command, although he said nothing.

Kacie had her hand on the door handle when Jake brought the car to a smooth stop. But the thing wouldn't open, no matter how hard she tugged. It was locked, no doubt, by a master switch on his side.

Jake's large hand on her shoulder stilled her struggles. "Oh no, Irish," he rebuked. "I'll see you to your door."

She faced him in the velvet shadows. "That isn't necessary, Jake. You've done quite enough for me for one evening," she disagreed with sarcastic emphasis.

"Not nearly as much as I'm going to do," he growled on a hardening note. He slid out of the car and came around to her side.

Knowing it was useless to protest further, Kacie allowed him to escort her into the hotel and to her room. He stood silently by while she fumbled for her key.

When she had opened the door, she turned to dismiss him.

"Not just yet, Kacie," he murmured, using one muscled arm to push the panel wider to admit his broad frame.

Kacie gave way before his determination. She heard the lock click shut with a sense of fatalism. She stood rooted to the middle of the floor, her eyes wide. She watched helplessly as Jake took two measured steps forward until he was only inches away. She felt anger emanating from him as waves of sensation over her skin. He seemed to fill her room, blocking out the sight and sound of everything but him. Her own temper finally rose in challenge. She was the injured party, not he. It was *her* right to be steaming mad. All the Irish fury he attributed to her surged to the fore. She threw her handbag at the sofa.

"Damn you, Jake. What right have you to force yourself in here?" she demanded wrathfully.

Jake's ebony eyes became slits of emotion at her tone. His hands shot out, biting into her bare shoulders with fingers of steel. He shook her twice. "Force my way! Good Lord, woman," he raged furiously. "I've spent weeks trying to get close to you, damn it, and you dress up like a tart for another man!"

"Tart!" Kacie yelped. *"Tart?* Why, you arrogant, overbearing bully. I bought this blasted dress to wear last night . . . with you!"

Jake shook her again, more roughly, ignoring her struggle to free herself. "Don't give me that! You bought that rag just to get back at me for not showing up." He hauled her against his chest, clamping her flailing arms at her sides. "Well, if you wanted to arouse me, you've damn well succeeded," he muttered harshly as his mouth descended.

Seeing his intention, Kacie squirmed frantically, seeking escape. There wasn't an ounce of tenderness in his embrace. The touch of his lips was an extension of his anger. He made no concession for her tender mouth. He demanded entrance into the dark cave, unmercifully bruising the soft skin.

Beyond fear of Jake's temper, knowing only the red rage of her own lacerated emotions, Kacie fought back with the only weapon at her disposal—her body. A vagrant thought showed her the way. Attack was the best form of defense. The ageless proverb was no sooner remembered than acted upon. She ceased her useless struggle and arched her soft curves fiercely against his hard muscles, hoping to lessen the strength of his on-slaught. Her tongue became a rapier that thrust and jabbed with all the expertise of a master swordsman. She was a woman embattled, and she used all the arsenals at her command to meet her foe. Her arms fought free of Jake's restraining fingers to wind around his broad shoulders as she drew him closer, absorbing the heavy weight of him against her softness.

But somehow the very act of meeting Jake as an equal triggered a deep need in her—a desire to make him know her as a woman and to bind him to her in any way possible. She wanted him, she needed him, but most of all, she loved him.

Her response set off a change in her adversary's ap-proach. The hard mouth gentled, ceasing its ravishing. The arms that held her lost their harsh roughness.

Sanity returned with a crash. She was appalled at her own self-betrayal. Taking advantage of the slackened hold, Kacie quickly pushed away. She was breathing heavily as she backed up to put a chair between them. She eyed him warily across the space separating them. Jake's breath heaved audibly in the silence, underlining her own soft panting. For a moment neither spoke.

Kacie saw the speculation in Jake's ebony stare. She sent up a fervent prayer to the Fates to open up a hole under her feet. She didn't need to see the dawning com-prehension in Jake's eyes to know she had betrayed her-self beyond all pretense.

Jake studied her, taking in the defensive attitude she maintained behind the shielding bulk of the chair. She knew her hair must have been in wild disorder about hectically flushed cheeks. Her silk-covered breasts rose and fell rapidly, damning indications of her response to him.

The last remnants of his anger and surprise seemed to melt away. He stepped forward, then stopped, watching her darting glance that sought escape.

"I won't pounce again, Irish," he coaxed quietly. "I promise."

Kacie stared at him, scarcely believing his sudden gentleness. She hesitated, torn between retreating and flying into his arms to find peace, even if only momentarily.

"Come on, Irish, I won't hurt you," he tried again. "I only want to hold you."

She shook her head, her grip tightening on the chair back.

"What are you afraid of? Me?" He watched her closely, his whole body tense, waiting for her answer. He got none. "Yourself?" he asked finally.

It never occurred to her to lie. She nodded, moistening her dry lips with the tip of her tongue. He knew it all now.

Jake sighed and ran a hand through his own rumpled hair. "Nothing is turning out right," he muttered ruefully. "I'll order us both some coffee, then you and I are going to have a talk. There is something here I don't understand at all. And I'll find out what it is if I have to stay in this room all night to do it."

"I don't want any coffee," Kacie objected wearily, speaking for the first time.

"You may not, but I do," he stated, heading for the phone. "Go sit down."

She stared at his retreating back, recognizing with dismay that no-nonsense tone of voice. Nothing or no

one would make a bit of difference in his search for the
answers he wanted. Short of physically ejecting him, she
had no alternative but to obey his command. She sank
into the chair that had been her bulwark against him,
feeling as though her legs would no longer support her.
Now that her anger had subsided, reaction was setting
in. She was tired, near the end of her endurance, and
she knew it. Jake had won. She stared at her hands in
her lap, too drained to lift her head at his approach. When
his fingers reached down and took her icy ones in his
warm grasp, she didn't struggle.

"Come on over to the sofa," Jake directed, pulling
her to her feet. As she swayed, he put an arm around
her waist to steady her. There was no seduction in his
touch, only a firm strength that asked nothing in return
for the support being offered. Kacie leaned against him
as he led her to the couch.

"Are you all right?" he asked in concern, evidently
noting the pallor she felt.

She nodded, then leaned her head back and closed her
eyes. She welcomed the black cocoon of darkness, drift-
ing in a calm sea of blessed silence. She knew Jake had
taken a seat beside her, but even that had no power to
touch her. She sensed his restraint while he waited for
the coffee to arrive.

The muted rattle of china and silverware brought her
eyes open, and she watched Jake smoothly tip and dismiss the room-service waiter.

"Here, drink this." He handed her a cup of black
coffee, holding it only long enough to be sure she had
a good grip on the handle.

It was easier to do as he said than to argue. Kacie
sipped carefully, feeling the reviving warmth spread

through her, dispelling some of the chill.

Jake waited until she placed her empty cup back onto the tray before he spoke. His body was turned toward her so he could see her expression clearly.

"Am I the first man who has ever gotten to you?" he asked bluntly. "Before you answer, hear me out. I know you're not immune to me, so don't try telling me I'm imagining your responses. What I don't understand is your constant retreat every time I try to get close to you. If you had been married or badly hurt, I could understand it." He caught the flash of remembered pain before Kacie could veil her eyes. "That's it!" he exclaimed on a low note of triumph. "Someone has hurt you?"

She heard the question seeking her confirmation or denial, and she firmed her lips rebelliously. Exhausted as she was, she had no intention of baring her life to his probing eyes.

Obviously recognizing her mutinous expression, Jake tried another approach. "Kacie, you admitted you were afraid of yourself. Don't you think that deserves some kind of explanation?" His voice was a soft, cajoling whisper pleading for a response.

"I owe you nothing, Jake," she denied with the last of her strength. "You're neither parent nor husband."

"Damn it, Kacie, I want you. Haven't I proved that much at least? Surely that gives me some rights," Jake demanded with opaque male logic in the face of her continued stubbornness.

She felt him willing her to answer, almost forcing the words he wanted to hear past her lips. Miraculously, he appeared not to have discovered the depths of her feeling for him. That fact, more than anything, made her give him the information he sought. Maybe if the Fates were kind, she might salvage her pride, if nothing else.

"You're good, Jake. I'll give you that," she told him
with bitter emphasis. "Your relentless hunt is finally over.
I can't fight any more." She shook her head tiredly. "I
was engaged once . . . while I was studying for my master's. Michael Blair was a guest lecturer in one of my
computer classes." She glared at Jake's intent face.
"Skipping the gory details, it didn't work out, mainly
because there was a cute blond he wanted more."

Jake reached out to touch her for the first time since
he'd sat down. She flinched away instinctively, only to
be drawn firmly into his arms until her breasts pressed
against his chest.

"Now tell me the gory details, Irish. Let's get it all
out now," he urged from somewhere above her ear.

Kacie lay quiescent against him, not actively responding to his embrace, yet drawing comfort from his solid
strength and the warmth of his body against hers. She
felt the soothing stroke of his hands along her back.
Suddenly she wanted to tell him, needed to cry out her
pain. Somehow she knew he would understand. Unable
to help herself, her arms encircled his waist and she
nestled closer to him. Her voice was muffled against his
shirt when she spoke.

"I met him soon after my parents were killed. I was
alone and lonely, and Michael was like a light in the
darkness. He was handsome, lively, yet serious, too, and
older. All the things a girl dreams of in a husband."
There was a distinct note of self-mockery in the last
statement. "School was important to me, and I thought
Michael knew that. I wanted to wait until I finished before
we married. It never occurred to me to wonder if he was
satisfied with our arrangement. I trusted him to tell me

the truth." She paused, gathering strength to relate the final betrayal. "I stopped by his apartment one afternoon, and I found him and Debbie in what is known as a compromising situation." She laughed, a harsh sound splintered with pain. "The funny part was, he said I wasn't woman enough for him—that I had driven him to her arms." She shuddered, recalling the awful scene. Jake's arms tightened like steel bands around her, and he swore an ugly oath.

"I hope you called him the name he deserved," Jake growled, his tone conveying all the disgust he felt for her former fiancé.

Kacie shook her head slightly. "I couldn't. I wanted to hide where no one could ever find me again."

"So you did the next best thing. You buried yourself alive in your work," Jake finished for her. With one hand he lifted her face away from his chest until he was staring down into her pain-filled eyes. "He wasn't worth it, Irish. The man was an insensitive bastard who didn't deserve a second thought. The only thing wrong was a slight error in judgment on your part for believing you loved him." He gazed at her, seemingly willing her to accept the truth of his words.

She saw the compassion in his eyes, felt the gentle, healing touch of his hands. Slowly the last lingering scars of her past ceased to ache. Whatever else he might do, Jake wouldn't lie.

She reached out her hand to lightly touch his cheek, feeling the soft rasp of stubble beneath her fingertips. Her heart filled with gratitude and love as she gazed into the ebony depths only inches away from her face.

The hand under her chin glided slowly down the white column of her neck, the fingers stroking the sensitive pulse in the hollow of her throat before deliberately tracing the smooth curve of each breast with a tantalizing, feather-soft caress.

Kacie watched, fascinated, as the dark velvet pools flared into flames of awakening desire. If he chose to take her there on the couch, she would not stop him. She was his as surely as if she had declared her love. She waited, scarcely breathing, for his kiss.

Jake lowered his head and gently brushed her slightly parted lips, then grinned at the look of disappointment she couldn't hide.

"You're tired, Irish, even if you don't know it." He eased her away from him until she leaned back against the cushions. "And believe it or not, I am too. I want you too much to make our first time together less than it should be." He held her gaze intently. "Do you understand what I'm saying? I still want you like hell. My bones ache with wanting you, but not this way. Not when you're exhausted and upset." He ran his fingers lightly over one pale cheek before withdrawing reluctantly. "I like your temper too much to see it quenched."

Tears gathered in Kacie's eyes at his gentleness. She had never loved him more. In a blurred mist she saw him rise to his feet and head for the door, where he paused, eyeing her still figure. "Will you be all right?"

She nodded, not trusting herself to speak. If she did, she might beg him to come back...to hold her...to make her his.

"I'll pick you up in the morning," he told her softly. "Dream of me, Irish."

The soft click of the door closing released the dam of tears. She cried not over Michael, but over Jake—the paradoxical giant who was at one and the same time ruthless pursuer and gentle man . . . She cried for the love she carried for this man who knew only desire for her. But most of all, she cried for the hopeless future. If giving herself to Michael brought pain, committing her soul to Jake would be ecstasy while it lasted—and sheer agony in hell when it ended.

7

"YUCK! I LOOK awful!" Kacie splashed more cold water on her already dripping face, then raised her head to peer into the mirror above the bathroom sink. She wrinkled her nose at the pale, blotchy image that stared back at her. She looked as terrible as she felt. Crying half the night was definitely not conducive to appearing at her best in the morning. She wished she dared call Jake and ask for the day off. For once, work held no appeal. She felt as fragile as glass and not in the least ready to cope with a recalcitrant computer.

Reaching for a towel, she dried her face and padded back to her bedroom. She stopped in front of her open closet, surveying its colorful contents with a jaundiced eye. Selecting a classic dress of soft gray and a silk scarf patterned with shades of blue, she quickly slipped the dress over her head, knotted the scarf at her throat, and sat down in front of the dressing table.

Blessing the impulse that had prompted her purchase of the complete line of famous cosmetics, she set about disguising the effects of her emotional night. When she was done, she eyed the finished product critically. The layers of base cream and powder felt stiff to her usually un-madeup face, but anything was better than what was underneath. Pulling a brush through her hair, she cast a quick glance at the clock. Jake should be arriving at any second.

Right on cue his knock sounded. The first words out of his mouth destroyed the image she had spent the last hour constructing.

"Spent the night crying, did you?" he remarked with devastating candor. He stepped forward, his hand pushing the door shut behind him. "If I had known you were going to do this to yourself, I would have stayed no matter what I . . ." He stopped mid-sentence, eyeing her warily.

Kacie stared at him, a blush rising in her cheeks at his piercing scrutiny. All morning she had purposefully avoided thinking about Jake. She felt raw and vulnerable where he was concerned. His withdrawal the night before had completely confused her. She knew a man of his experience couldn't have missed her unspoken surrender. Now his words . . . those he hadn't voiced . . . demanded an explanation.

"You what, Jake?" she asked, facing him across a foot of space. She tried to read his expression and failed. For a moment she was sure he wouldn't answer.

"Don't be obtuse," he replied impatiently. "We both know what could have happened last night."

Kacie nodded, past being embarrassed by his blunt words or by her own surrender. She wanted the truth, the key to this maze of emotions she was trapped in.

"Why did you leave?"

Jake stared at her, an expression of disbelief on his rugged face. He spanned the distance separating them until his hands firmly grasped her shoulder.

Kacie searched his ebony eyes.

"I left for exactly the reasons I told you. When we go to bed, together I want it to be because you want it as much as I do—*not* because you're too damned tired to fight any more," he enunciated slowly as though speaking to a child. He dropped his hands and took a step back. "Now, are you ready to go?" he asked, his voice losing its deep timbre.

Reacting to the change in his tone, she nodded, automatically picking up her bag. She walked silently beside him to the elevator. She had wanted the truth, and she had gotten it with a vengeance. For one insane moment she had hoped his sensitivity was due to more than his desire to possess her. His words had shattered that fantasy.

"Are you all right?" he asked as he slid into the driver's seat.

"I'm fine," she replied briefly.

"Good." He started the car. "Because Mark's get-together is tonight."

"Tonight?" Kacie echoed, startled. "Since when?"

Jake shot her a quick glance before directing his attention to the heavy traffic ahead. "Yesterday afternoon. I was going to tell you last night, but I got sidetracked."

Kacie ignored the end of his statement and concentrated on visualizing her limited wardrobe. She knew without being told that Jake would expect her to be dressed in something special. The only problem was that she hadn't bought any really dressy things.

"Long or short?"

"What?"

"Long gowns or short?" she elaborated patiently.

Jake shrugged, his shoulder brushing against her momentarily in the close confines of the bucket seats. "Long. Will that be a problem?"

She grimaced expressively. "I'm not sure," she admitted. "It depends on how formal a 'do' it is."

"Not terribly." He drove into the parking garage, pulled into the reserved VIP slot, and switched off the engine. He turned toward her, his eyes running assessingly over the gray linen dress she wore. His attention lingered for a moment on the elegant silk scarf encircling her throat.

"If it's similar to this"—he fingered the smooth fabric lightly—"then it will be perfect."

Kacie smiled at him, pleased at the oblique compliment. She hadn't forgotten his disapproval of her other purchase.

"Just so it's not like that pink dress," he added in a tone tinged with remembered anger.

"There wasn't a thing wrong with that garment," she retorted, annoyed. The way he acted, anyone would think it had been cut clear down to the navel.

"That's not the way I saw it, or John either," Jake stated flatly. "When I told you to come out of your shell, I didn't expect you to go to extremes."

Kacie opened her mouth to refute his unfair accusation, but the angry words in her mind were never uttered. Suddenly the odd tenseness about him, the harshness in his voice made sense. He was jealous. Jake was actually jealous. There was no other possible explanation for his unreasoning condemnation of the pink and lavender.

A faint flicker of hope was born. Where there was jealousy, there could be more than mere desire. Not necessarily love, but an attraction deeper than just physical need.

"I didn't buy anything else remotely like that style," she finally offered. "I promise you you won't find anything to object to in the gown I plan to wear."

For a moment Jake appeared stunned by her ready acquiescence to his dictates. He eyed her uncertainly. "I won't?"

"No."

Unexpectedly, Jake grinned, looking years younger. "I can't believe you're not arguing with me."

Kacie laughed, her sense of humor surfacing at his astonishment. Considering their past skirmishes, she could see his point. "Hadn't we better get going?" she asked, indicating the time.

"Definitely—especially since I'm winning," he teased, clearly enjoying her amusement.

"Only temporarily," she shot back, getting out of the car. Suddenly her perfectly disastrous morning was full of promise.

Even the sight of John's worried frown when she entered the lab alone couldn't dim her good mood.

"What's up?" she asked, slipping into her white coat.

John lifted his head from the printout sheets he was holding. "We've hit another snag."

Kacie moved calmly to his side. "Not the same place?" she queried, referring to the problem of the day before.

He shook his head. "No, farther along. Our friend appears to believe we're giving him contradictory instructions," he murmured dryly, indicating the computer. He pointed to the trouble spot in the printouts.

Kacie studied the figures in silence. "I thought this section had been cleared, ready for a new set of directions," she commented.

"It was, but I didn't think this would interfere with Jake's additions." John's expression revealed his irritation at his error in judgment.

Kacie shrugged lightly. "So let's clear this whole lot and put in the new procedure. The sooner we begin . . ."

John's face smoothed at her easy attitude, and he grinned slightly. "This doesn't seem to be my week for making smart decisions."

Kacie quirked a brow in mute question.

"Last night was a . . ." He stopped, evidently sensing her withdrawal at the mention of their date.

"Last night?" she repeated coolly. Now it would come. The probing into the situation between her and Jake. She regretted her momentary loss of her businesslike approach with John.

"Will you and Jake . . ." His voice trailed to a stop. John looked distinctly uncomfortable. Apparently he couldn't finish what he had started to say.

"I think we both ought to concentrate on Jake's system and forget about last night," she suggested in a tone that didn't invite any further questions.

Nodding, he accepted her reprimand.

The rest of the morning passed quickly. John and Kacie worked silently side by side. The easy rapport of the day before was gone. Having retreated into her cool efficiency, Kacie was very definitely the boss. John recognized the change and responded accordingly.

It was nearing noon, and they still had a bit to do. Jake had told her they were going out for lunch. She was supposed to be ready by twelve. Not wanting to leave in the middle of the job, she picked up the phone and quickly dialed his office.

His deep growl was abrupt as he answered. "Weston."

A fleeting smile touched Kacie's lips at the snapped off greeting. How typical of him.

"Jake, it's me," she began hurriedly, knowing he was probably as busy as she.

Jake's rich chuckle sounded in her ear, interrupting her before she could explain why she'd called.

"Hello, me. I hope this conversation doesn't mean our date is off." There wasn't a trace of Jake the boss in his manner.

His voice was intimately warm against her ear, sending shivers of pleasure down her spine. She was glad John had stepped out for a minute. The last thing she needed was for him to witness the color she felt staining her cheeks.

"Not exactly," she replied, striving to disguise the effect his teasing voice was having on her. "We've run into a small hang-up. I'd like to clear it up before we leave."

She heard the rustle of pages turning in the background. "How long do you think it will take?"

"An hour and a half . . . two at the most."

"No problem. I could use the extra time myself." He hesitated for a split second. "How about if you come up here at two? I should be finished by then."

"Okay." She started to hang up the phone, but Jake's voice stopped her.

"Don't be late, or I'll come and get you."

Kacie stared at the receiver in her hand as the dial tone cut off the sound of Jake's low rumble of laughter. A week ago she would have slammed the receiver back into its cradle with an angry bang. Now she laid it gently to rest with a curious little smile curving her lips. The teasing note in Jake's tone hadn't completely masked the underlying seriousness of his threat. Something feminine in Kacie responded to the possessive demand.

It took a conscious effort on her part to concentrate on the last stages of the program remaining to be completed. She worked swiftly, knowing Jake would make good his promise if she wasn't waiting for him. Promptly at one forty-five she slipped out of her coat and collected her handbag. The computer was once again functioning properly. Leaving John to double-check their work, she headed for Jake's office.

She silently entered the outer room of Jake's suite and stopped in front of the secretary's desk. The well-groomed woman presiding raised her head and smiled politely.

"May I help you?"

"I'm Kacie Daniels. Mr. Weston is expecting me."

The woman's impersonal attitude thawed slightly as she nodded. "Oh, yes. He said to send you right in." She gestured toward the closed panel to her right.

Thanking her, Kacie crossed the floor and opened the door. Behind her she could feel the secretary's eyes following her movements. That made twice today that her private life had intruded on her business. She didn't like the thought of the speculation that was bound to arise when word got out about her supposed relationship with Jake. She hadn't forgotten how often his name figured in the home office gossip. She wasn't pleased at the prospect of being listed as his "latest."

"You look ruffled." Jake's deep voice cut into her thoughts. "Why don't you come on in and shut the door," he invited, making Kacie aware she had stopped just over the threshold.

"Sorry," she apologized quickly. "I was miles away."

Jake rose from behind the desk and came around to meet her as she moved into the room. "Didn't you get your problem squared away?" he asked as he halted before her.

She had to tilt her head back to meet Jake's eyes. She shrugged lightly. "That's all ironed out." She saw his eyes narrow.

"Has someone upset you?" he questioned, his expression telling her he meant to have an answer. "John?"

She shook her head. "What could he say?"

"Plenty... I know I would in his shoes," he replied. He reached out and grasped her shoulders. "Did he?"

Kacie's eyes widened at the intensity of his probing. It obviously bothered him to think that John might have said something. A gentle shake reminded her he was waiting.

"No more than I could handle," she admitted finally.

"You're sure?" One dark brow rose in an imperious demand.

"Aren't we going to eat?" Kacie felt the inquisition had gone on long enough. Heaven only knew what Jake's secretary thought about their delayed departure.

Fighting the feelings coursing through her, she sought to put some distance between her and the source of her emotional chaos. Then she was unreasonably piqued when Jake released her so promptly. Those few seconds of physical contact had sparked off sensations difficult to resist. The urge to lean against the solid length of him had her curling her nails into her palms in an effort to control her weakness. The sooner they were out of the office and away from the watching eyes of the staff, the better.

Jake touched her arm lightly. "Ready?"

She nodded, then stepped through the door he opened for her. She stood quietly at his side when he stopped in front of the outer desk.

"I may not be back this afternoon. If there's anything urgent, refer it to Dave," he directed, naming the office vice president.

With a sinking feeling in the pit of her stomach, Kacie saw the knowing look cast discreetly in her direction. She knew Jake had seen it, too, by the way he glanced her way. Her eyes lit with anger at his blatant actions. Why hadn't he just shouted his intentions to the world? It would've saved a lot of people the trouble of relaying his plans.

By the time they reached the car, Kacie was seething with anger, hurt, and confusion. Where was the gentle, sensitive man she'd thought was Jake? She knew that little episode was staged for a purpose, but what? Surely he didn't mean to humiliate her because of her resistance to him. No, she wouldn't believe that of him. Jake might be ruthless when he wanted something, but he wasn't cruel.

"You're very quiet," he commented as he slid into the car beside her. "Something wrong?"

She turned her head, finding his eyes fixed unwaveringly on her face. "Why, Jake? Why did you do it?" She knew her expression reflected her confusion.

Jake trailed one finger along the line of her jaw to her ear, where he tucked a stray curl behind the lobe in a possessive gesture. "Why do you think?" he asked huskily.

Kacie Mutely stared at him. Doubts filled her mind, yet near him like this she was incapable of voicing a single one of them. She passed her tongue over her dry lips. "I don't know," she whispered finally. The stroke of Jake's finger against the side of her neck was sending strange quivers through her. Her mind shut itself off to the outside world. She saw only his rugged face so close to her own; felt only the touch of his hand, the pressure of his thigh against hers. His voice was a velvet caress. It was broad daylight in a crowded parking garage, yet it might well have been midnight on a deserted beach.

"You're mine, Kacie. I wanted everyone to know it, including you," he stated quietly, watching her reaction to his words closely.

"We haven't even . . ." she objected helplessly.

"Made love?" His other hand came up to frame her face. "Does it matter?" he asked softly just before his lips covered hers, blotting out whatever answer she might have made.

She would have said it mattered a great deal, but the sensuous movement of Jake's mouth on hers robbed her of anything except a desire to respond in kind. She melted against him, feeling the buttons of his suit pressing through the thin fabric of her dress. Her hands slid across his shoulders to tangle in the thick dark hair at the nape of his neck, where they gripped with feminine strength. She was lost in a sea of sensations as his tongue probed her mouth in a provocative imitation of the love act. She arched closer in response to the pressure of his cradling arms. Her own arms tightened to bind him to her. When she felt his withdrawal, she instinctively moaned her protest.

"Shh, Irish," he murmured against her lips. The caressing stroke of his hands soothed the flame he had ignited. Kacie opened passion-drugged eyes to stare at the flaming ebony depths of his.

"I didn't mean for that to happen," he commented on a light note, which didn't disguise the husky timbre indicating his own aroused state. "I should have known better."

She knew he was talking to give her time to come down from the high plane he'd transported her to. He still held her, though lightly now.

"Well, it wasn't my idea," she reminded him in a voice fast returning to normal.

"I suppose not." Jake pulled his arms away with marked reluctance. "Why is it that all but one of our encounters have taken place in a car?" he mused idly, his eyes lingering on her lips.

Trying to subdue the desire still smoldering within her, Kacie concentrated on his words.

"Maybe because you're always on the go," she suggested hopefully.

"Or because you feel safer," he countered swiftly with a direct look that dared her to deny his assessment.

"Are you going to feed me or not?" she demanded.

Grinning at her saucy question, Jake turned and started the engine. "I am—right now."

Kacie leaned back in her seat, trying to relax. Closing her eyes, she let her mind dwell on Jake's words. His statement about their encounters in cars had hit too close to the truth. She was well aware of her vulnerability where Jake was concerned. Not only did she love him, but he touched her on a physical level no man had ever reached before. She wanted him more with each passing day. She knew, too, that soon she would be his. But would he be hers? Could she, in whatever time remained before that final commitment, come to mean more to him than just another desirable female? Could want grow into love? His possessive attitude, his jealousy, hinted at more. Did she dare believe it could be so?

"Are we going back to your favorite seafood place?" she asked, breaking the silence between them. She'd noticed the direction they were taking.

Jake shook his head. "When you called, I had my secretary cancel our reservations."

"I hope she was able to fit us in somewhere else." Kacie saw his lips twitch, and she was instantly suspicious. "It's not the local hamburger stand?"

"Wait and see." He flashed her a quick grin. "I promise you you'll be fed."

"I hope so," she replied tartly. "I'm beginning to feel starved." In more ways than one, she honestly admitted to herself, covertly staring at him. Was it only seconds ago that he had held her in his arms? There was only the slightest trace of that Jake now. Or was she being supersensitive, looking for that special, deep, growling quality in his voice to indicate his response to her?

The sudden dimness in place of the brilliantly sunny sky overhead drew her startled attention from her study. She glanced around, realizing they had entered an underground parking area.

"Where are we?" she asked, noticing the numbered slots among the spaces.

For a moment Jake didn't answer as he guided his car to a stop in one marked PH. "My penthouse," he stated calmly, extracting the keys from the ingition. Without waiting for her comment, he opened his door and got out.

Sheer surprise made Kacie copy his actions. "Why?" she asked, following him to the elevator only a few feet away. "Have you forgotten something?"

"No." The doors silently slid open, and he gestured for her to precede him. "My place doesn't require reservations.

"We're eating here?" Kacie clarified slowly.

Evidently struck by the odd note in her tone, Jake studied her thoughtfully. "What's the matter, Irish? Afraid to be alone with me?"

Kacie found her eyes drawn to his face. She swallowed, unable to voice any of her confusing emotions. "Should I be?" she asked in an attempt at lightness that didn't quite succeed.

Jake shook his head. "Oh, Irish. What am I going to do with you . . . all fiery woman one minute and bewildered child the next." He stood beside her in the small compartment, not touching her. Then, with a smile, he took her hand in his large grasp, completely enveloping the fine bones. "You know you're safe with me," he murmured in a deepening rumble of male assurance while his ebony eyes searched her worried face.

Responding as much to the timbre of his voice as to the man, Kacie swayed toward the source of her confusion. She knew in her heart that he spoke the truth. He might tease her, provoke her, and kiss her until the world faded away, but he had never harmed her. Her doubts fell away.

Jake allowed her one brief embrace before the doors slid noiselessly open. "Come on, woman. I'm hungry," he teased, tugging her behind him by the hand he still held.

She had no choice but to follow his lead. Even if she wanted to refuse, which she didn't, she wouldn't have had an opportunity.

Jake's apartment was a total surprise. Expecting a

place still in the throes of being renovated for occupancy, Kacie was confronted with a complete setting for the man she was coming to know. The first thing she noticed was the extraordinary deep pile shag carpet cloaking the floors. A rich dark brown, it had the look and feel of lush fur. She found her toes itching to sink into the thick pelt. Large windows and sky-blue walls brought the open airiness of the outdoors to the arrangements of traditionally styled mahogany and overstuffed furniture. The whole apartment radiated space, freedom, and relaxation.

"You can take your shoes off," Jake murmured with a grin when they had completed a tour of the rooms.

"Was I that obvious?" Kacie smiled, finding it remarkably easy to follow his suggestion. She wriggled her toes appreciatively, then laughed out loud when Jake discarded his own footwear.

"I have a feeling there was a method to your madness," she couldn't help teasing.

"Always, Irish, didn't you know?" The seriousness of his gaze belied the good-humored reply. Bending his head, he brushed her parted lips with a brief, hard kiss.

"Jake?" Kacie's question hovered softly between their lips. She swayed closer to him until their bodies touched. She wanted to feel his arms around her.

"M-m-m?" Jake pressed his frame against her soft curves, but still he made no move to hold her.

Her senses flaring alive under the potent effect of his rugged masculinity, Kacie felt a growing frustration at his continued distancing. With a groan of surrender, she arched fiercely into him, her arms sliding around his shoulders, her mouth reaching hungrily for his.

"I thought you were starved?" he whispered in a husky growl a split second before their lips met.

I am, Kacie moaned in her mind as Jake's strong arms wrapped around her, feeding the burning desire fast blazing out of control.

No gentle wooing this. For too long she had fought her attraction to Jake. His caresses had left her with a steadily growing need for the fulfillment he promised— a need she'd been barely conscious of until recently. Oh, she'd known she wanted him, loved him. But this raging thirst for his touch was a revelation.

Twining herself around his strong, muscled length like a vine clinging to the sturdy oak, Kacie whispered to him of her desire. Depending on him to support them both, she slid one stocking-clad limb up and down his leg in a sensuous, stroking motion that drew a groan of response from her giant. Excited by the evidence of her appeal, she explored his back and hips with urgent, searching fingers. His jacket hampered her quest, and she pulled at it fretfully.

Suddenly the room spun dizzily as Jake, his mouth never leaving hers, swung her into his arms. She barely had time to adjust to this new position before she felt the cloudlike softness of Jake's bed beneath her. Her black hair sprayed out across the pillows like a dark fan. Jake lifted his head to gaze down at her, and she felt a flush of mounting desire invade her cheeks.

"God, you're beautiful, Irish," he muttered hoarsely, drawing his thumb across her lips.

Her wide eyes fastened on his face. She flicked the tip of her tongue between her lips to taste the soft pad as it made another sweep.

"Don't do that!" Jake commanded in a tortured whisper, staring at her with male need mirrored in his eyes. His shoulders loomed over her, sheltering her. "I'm trying to remember it's our first time."

Kacie's eyes widened even more at his words. Was that why he was holding back? Didn't he know yet how much she wanted him?

"I want you, Jake," she whispered achingly. "Now."

Her breathless demand seemed to loosen the restraint he was exercising. With a groan he lowered his weight onto her yielding softness, his hands coming up to frame her face.

"I've waited forever to hear you say it, Kacie. I was beginning to think I'd have to take what I wanted."

Uncomprehending, Kacie stared at him. "Take?" she questioned dazedly. She was so intent on his lips forming the words, she scarcely noticed one hand moving to the scarf at her throat and untying it.

He nodded. "I've wanted you from the beginning, but you weren't about to come out of your shell," he grinned, self-satisfaction lighting his eyes. "At least not until I teased you a bit." He rolled over onto his back, pulling her on top of him. Her hair hung like a curtain on either side of her face and brushed over Jake's chest.

"I'm out now," she commented in a breathy whisper.

"Not quite," he replied, his free hand finding her dress zipper and sliding it down to the base of her spine, "but almost."

With the release of the fastener, the sheath slipped easily over her shoulders to reveal her soft breasts cupped in a sheer, lacy bra. The hardened rosy peaks showed clearly through the filmy mesh, drawing Jake's eyes. The snap clip was expertly released with one deft movement, and the bra was discarded.

Kacie caught her breath at the naked hunger that flared in the ebony depths of Jake's eyes. Suddenly she could wait no longer. With fingers that trembled, she removed his tie, then unbuttoned his shirt. She tugged the edges open, heedless of the fine fabric, to reveal a dark pelt of thick, curly hair. Sensuously gliding downward along his body, she pressed her bare breasts into the rough curls on his chest.

Jake's reaction was instantaneous. The slow deliberation of his movements ceased abruptly, and his hand reached out to wrap itself in her tangled hair, locking her head still for his kiss.

Kacie was made to know of the desire she had unleashed in him. He didn't seek permission to enter her mouth, but invaded it at once. Her only wish at that moment was to satisfy, to give, as she let her emotions run free for the first time with a man. Jake stroked her whole body, removing the last bits of clothing as he did. Trembling beneath the burning touch of his palms, she reached out to explore his masculine form, letting the tips of her fingers telegraph the delight she found in the rugged contours. Clothes showered to the floor as she followed the line of his rib cage down to the tautness of his flat stomach and beyond. It seemed her mind and body, having finally burst the walls surrounding them, were intent on exploring every pleasure known to man and woman. Her lips trailed across the sandpaper rasp of his jaw down the brown throat to the hardened male nipples. She barely had a chance to taste the treasures she found.

With a powerful roll Jake turned them over, trapping her beneath him. "You're an Irish witch," he muttered hoarsely against her lips before moving down her neck to the soft globes of fullness beyond.

"Jake," she moaned in response to the heat of his mouth as it enclosed an erect rosy peak. "Oh, yes, Jake!" Her hands clenched convulsively around the muscles of his buttocks and then traveled up the sinewy back to cling to his shoulders as she arched against his sucking lips.

Jake reacted as if she had set a torch to his already flaming desire. One powerful thigh forced its way between hers. Instantly she surrendered to the invasion. With each caress Jake sought more. No longer a patient lover, he demanded responses from her, giving her no breathing space, no time to savor each small surrender leading up to the final yielding.

Kacie arched her hips against his stroking hand as he found the sensitive inner source of her desire. Deeper and deeper his hand moved until he knew beyond a shadow of doubt of her readiness.

"Jake!" she groaned, feeling tension building within her. She was climbing a mountain, the peak was just ahead. She had to reach ... she had to ...

"Jake, take me now, please," she begged hoarsely, her breath soft gasps of unfulfilled need.

With a hungry growl, Jake rose briefly above her and then settled firmly between her thighs.

For a stunned instant, Kacie went still at the shock of his entry, then she felt him begin to move inside her. He covered her mouth with his, his tongue duplicating the motions of his body in an erotic rhythm that permeated her being. One large hand cupped her buttocks while the other caressed a breast. Kacie felt as though she had been absorbed into the mighty strength of him, inhaled into his blood. Dizzy with sensation, she clung to him.

"I love you," she moaned incoherently.

"You're mine," he rasped. His hand dug into her hips, lifting her for the final thrust.

The explosion was all Kacie had ever imagined. A

bursting of a dam, an uncontrollable release that was made even more incredible by the knowledge that Jake's had been right alongside hers.

It was a long time before she could stir from the warm haven of his embrace. When she did, she couldn't restrain a smile at the triumphant look on her lover's face.

"I'm still waiting for my lunch," she teased breathlessly, nipping gently at the shoulder beneath her head.

"Funny, I thought we'd already had it," Jake murmured. He managed to dodge the playful fist aimed at his jaw.

With a contented sigh, he dropped a kiss on her parted lips, his hand running possessively over one smooth hip before he released her.

"Come on, woman. Let's eat."

8

KACIE EMERGED FROM her shower, tingling from the warm spray against her sensitive skin. While she dried herself with a fluffy, chocolate-colored towel, she couldn't help but see her image in the mirrored wall dominating the masculine bath. She hardly recognized her reflection. Those moments in Jake's arms had changed her forever. But now what?

"Food's on, Irish. Are you about done?" Jake's deep rumble sounded from the bedroom, startling her into action.

"I'm coming..." Her voice trailed to a stop as she realized she didn't have a thing to put on with her. Darn Jake for pushing her in here anyway. Not that he could help the business call that had interrupted them on their way to the kitchen. "Jake, could you hand me my clothes?" she called finally.

"Why?"

She jumped at the impatient question from the other side of the door. Whipping the damp bath sheet around her bare form sarong style, she pulled open the door, finding Jake just about to do the same. "Because I can't sit down to eat like this," she muttered into his bare chest. She found it surprisingly hard to meet his eyes. He might be used to women parading around in towels, but she wasn't used to being one who did.

"Shy, Irish?" Jake questioned with gentle humor.

Kacie nodded, her tousled hair tumbling about her bare shoulders.

Jake's hand under her chin forced her head up. "I thought we had finally smashed that shell of yours to bits," he murmured softly.

"Dented it a little," she amended ruefully, staring into his eyes. The understanding she saw there gave her the courage to try to express some of her anxiety. "I'm not . . ." she gestured helplessly with one slim arm.

With his free hand, Jake caught her fingers and brought them to his chest, pressing them against the dark pelt of hair. "Not accustomed to a man in your bedroom . . . er . . . his bedroom? Right?"

Kacie's lips curved into a tiny, grateful smile. "Yes." She felt his fingers slide along her jaw line in a soothing motion that had a curiously calming effect on her troubled mind.

"Why don't you get dressed. Then we'll eat before the food gets cold." He grinned at the surprise in her expression; then his face took on a serious mien. He shook his head admonishingly. "I'm not an insensitive young buck, you know. We've got all the time we want. I'm not going to push you into anything—and that includes my bed. Not that I wouldn't enjoy another sample of that delectable little carcass of yours," he added with a teasing leer as he released her. He headed for the door, leaving her staring after him.

"Ten minutes," he ordered without turning around.

Kacie used two of those minutes staring at the closed bedroom door. Every time she thought she knew Jake, he showed her a different side to his personality. How many men would have realized her feelings of shyness after the intimacy they had just shared? Moreover, an intimacy she had initiated! Damned few. For a man whose emotional vocabulary listed the words *want, need,* and *desire* and never *love,* he was surprisingly tuned in to her thoughts and emotions.

Still puzzling over Jake's ability to read her so well, Kacie slowly moved across the room to the neat stack of clothes on the end of the bed—further evidence of the gentle giant's caring. Her bra, panties, and stockings lay nicely folded next to her gray sheath. Even her scarf was squared and placed beside the lingerie. Rousing herself, she quickly donned everything but her shoes, which were still in the living room.

Jake was waiting for her with two glasses of white wine in his hands when she came out. "I thought you might enjoy this," he explained, offering her the chilled crystal.

"M-m-m, lovely." She took a thirsty sip. "How did you know?"

He shrugged, gesturing her toward the table in the window alcove overlooking the lake. "I don't know, I just did."

Kacie surveyed the attractively arranged lunch with an appreciative eye. "Is that New England clam chowder

I smell?" she asked as she took her seat.

"It is," he affirmed. "I thought since we're eating so late and we have Mark's dinner tonight, you'd prefer a light meal," he commented, taking his place across from her. "I seem to remember your having a fondness for it." A dark brow raised in question.

"One of my favorites." She laughed lightly. "I'm beginning to worry about how well you read me.

Jake looked up from serving her a bowlful from the large porcelain tureen in the center of the table. "There's no need. I told you once before I would never hurt you."

Kacie's amusement died. "Even the best intentions don't always work the way we wish."

Jake placed his own steaming chowder carefully in front of him. "That sounds like a warning," he stated quietly, his eyes watchful on her grave face.

She was silent for a moment. She desperately wanted a deeper commitment from Jake than just an occasional sleeping arrangement. But how could she explain herself?

"You think too much, Kacie." Jake's deep voice cut the quiet. "You can't spend your life planning every move like a computer program. Let yourself live."

"Be your bed partner, you mean," she replied sharply.

Jake's dark eyes glinted at her words. "Is that how you see our relationship?" he demanded grimly.

Kacie felt the building anger in him, and she could have cried for the loss of their earlier rapport. Yet she couldn't back down now. She wasn't built to handle the kind of intimacy he suggested. Old-fashioned and out of date as it was, it was still the way she felt.

"What else can I think?" she asked.

"I could shake you, do you know that?" Jake growled

dangerously. "How about viewing it as a relationship between two consenting *adults*"—he stressed the last word clearly—"one of whom professes to love the other."

"That was cruel, Jake," Kacie protested as she started to get up.

His hand shot out and grabbed her before she could escape. "Is it, Kacie? Why? Because I won't let you scurry back into that shell of yours? Because I won't let you go back to being a breathing computer instead of the vibrant woman you are?"

"Why should you care? You don't love me." Kacie fought back, goaded beyond endurance by the brutally honest assessment of the safe little world she had created since college and Michael's defection.

Jake shook her hand roughly, making her glad that was all he was holding.

"Damn it, who even knows what love is? I don't. Neither do you. You said you loved Michael, and look what happened."

"That wasn't my doing . . ."

Jake ignored her interruption. "I thought I loved Caroline. That sure as hell didn't work."

Kacie was struck dumb at the mention of Jake's ex-wife. He had never once spoken her name before.

"I care about you. Can't you accept that?" he asked. A persuasive, almost pleading, quality replaced the angry harshness when he spoke of his marriage.

Kacie stared at him, uncertain and doubtful, but caught in the velvet richness of his ebony gaze. She wanted to accept it. Oh, how she wanted to. Logic and her brain told her she was a fool, but her heart ignored their counsel.

"Yes," she stated simply, turning the hand he held

palm up in surrender. The warmth of his fingers closing gently around it sealed the bond between them.

"Now eat your lunch," Jake ordered softly.

Surprisingly, Kacie found it easy to do just that. The food was perfect. The chowder was thick and creamy, exactly the way she liked it. With the light, dry white wine and crusty French bread warm from the oven, it made a delectable late lunch.

The small blow-up between them had somehow cleared the air. Any lingering traces of awkwardness were gone. Jake's light banter and easy conversation stimulated Kacie's own wit.

"About last night?" There was a distinct note of challenge in her softly spoken words.

Jake's lips twisted in a crooked grin, his ebony eyes alight with mischief. "I was wondering when you'd get to that."

She raised an eyebrow expressively. "Good. Then explain," she decreed sternly. The judgmental effort she was striving for was spoiled by the laughter she felt spilling into her eyes. She didn't care how Jake had found her and John . . . now.

"Simple, really. I overheard John telling someone where he was taking you."

Kacie's mouth curved in a slight smile at his expression of male satisfaction. "You would have been up the proverbial creek without a paddle if you hadn't eavesdropped," she couldn't resist taunting with a giggle.

He shook his head. "Don't you believe it, Irish. I'll always know where you are." The teasing answer carried an underlying seriousness, which Kacie heard and responded to.

A shaft of pleasure shot through her at the possessive ring of his reply. "Is that a threat or a promise?"

Jake's black-velvet gaze caught and held her eyes. "You choose," he growled with soft emphasis.

A growing hope Kacie hardly dared name held her silent under his intense stare. Was his *care* another word for love? She desperately wanted to believe it was so.

"I choose promise," she murmured softly.

With her answer, Kacie was rewarded by a look of such tenderness that it stayed with her long after Jake had dropped her back at her hotel.

She had just three hours to transform herself from the working Kacie to the butterfly Irish of Jake's imagination.

The first thing on the agenda was deciding which of the three dresses she had purchased fit her requirements for the evening. Keeping in mind Jake's comments on the bluish-gray, which, on a whim, she had included in her case, she studied her closet. A flash of light blue caught her eye just as she was reaching for the rose wool crepe she had chosen. Impulsively, she pulled the forgotten purchase out.

The soft folds of the shimmering periwinkle-blue panne velvet flowed like a misty cloud from the hanger. Suddenly she knew that this was the dress. She could even wear the strappy little sandals she had bought to go with the blue and silver.

A smile curved her lips at the thought of Jake's reaction. The demure cowl neck and cap sleeves were just the look he'd said he wanted. She turned the dress around to survey the back. She nearly laughed aloud at the deep, draped scoop, which she remembered stopped at her waistline. Classically simple, it was still surprisingly sexy. The promise of innocence from the front and the temptation of experience in the exposure at the back.

While she filled the tub with warm water and the

crystals for a milk bath, she wondered briefly how many guests would be present at Mark's home. Recalling Abbey's descriptions of the palatial estate in Lake Forest, she decided the gathering would be quite large. Mark Stratton, it seemed, didn't do things on a small scale.

As she slipped into the cloudy water, her thoughts took a whole new direction. The silken caress of the warm liquid over her skin conjured up images of Jake's hands gliding possessively over her curves. While the heat soothed away the tiny aches left from their lovemaking, the vivid memory of their intimacy fired her blood. She was shocked at her need for him. She hated the hours separating them. He was like a fever burning within her.

Her desire increased as the time for him to arrive drew near. She scarcely noticed putting her makeup on. After highlighting her eyes with iridescent lavender shadow, which made them appear larger and more deeply sapphire than ever, she stroked on a pearlized rose lip gloss. Her lashes needed no embellishment, their dark fan shapes being naturally thick and lush. Knowing how much Jake liked her hair down, Kacie chose to brush it all tumbled to one side, securing it there with a peacock-plumed comb. The result was strikingly exotic as the royal blue of the miniature feather eyes against her black hair echoed the brilliant sapphire of her own.

Stepping into her gown, she slid it up to cover her bare breasts. Having no back meant wearing no bra, although there was a soft, silky bit of nothing stitched into the bodice to replace it. She twirled slowly in front of the full-length mirror, enjoying the fluid swirl of fragile velvet around her legs. The gown was all she had hoped it would be. The long clean lines embraced her slender figure like a lover, outlining each curve and revealing the petal-soft bare skin with exquisite expertise.

The sound of Jake's distinctive knock provided the crowning touch as a delicate blush of eager anticipation crept into her creamy cheeks. Without another glance at the mirror she floated to the door.

"I'm sorry I'm la—" Jake stopped mid-word in his explanation as he took in the vision of Kacie's loveliness. His eyes darkened possessively.

Kacie's welcoming smile faltered in the face of his stunned silence. "Don't you like it?"

Jake shook his head as though to clear it. "Like it?" he questioned, stepping forward and closing the door behind him. "Woman, that doesn't begin to describe how I feel." His hands slid up her bare arms as he pulled her close. "I'm going to spoil your lipstick, you know," he murmured just before his lips covered hers.

This was what she'd been waiting for all afternoon. She arched against him, opening her mouth to admit his probing tongue. She wrapped her arms around him as he pulled her tight against his chest. She was lost in the clean taste of him and the male scent of his skin, feasting like a starving woman at a banquet.

Suddenly she felt him stiffen in her arms, tearing his mouth from hers in an abrupt gesture.

"What the hell?" he demanded in an ominous growl.

Startled and confused, Kacie stared at him.

"Turn around," he commanded, his eyes glinting dangerously. When she made no immediate move to do as he said, Jake firmly took her by the shoulders and did it for her. There was a long silence as he stared at her completely exposed back.

Kacie swallowed, irritated at her own nervousness

over his reaction. She wriggled ineffectually, trying to escape the steely fingers holding her in place.

"You're not wearing this," he stated finally.

She glanced over her shoulder, the light of battle in her eyes. "Why not?"

"Because . . . because . . ."—Jake paused— "Because I won't have it," he growled at last. He released her quickly. "Now go change." He gave her a little push in the direction of her bedroom.

Kacie took two steps forward, then turned to face him, her hands on her hips. "Now listen, Jake Weston, I . . . am . . . not . . . changing. There is absolutely nothing wrong with this dress."

"Nothing wrong!" he roared in outrage. "My God, I've seen more clothes than that at a French beach."

"That's not true, and you know it," she swiftly retaliated.

Jake clenched his fists at his sides, obviously fighting for control. "Be reasonable, Irish. The thing hasn't any back. Aren't you afraid it'll slip or something?" he pointed out with male logic.

"No, I'm not afraid it will slip or something," she echoed sarcastically. "It just survived your bear hug. And even if it did," she rushed on, heedless of the darkening anger in his eyes, "you're big enough to protect my virtue."

"Damn it, Kacie, you make me sound like some kind of guardian."

"That's how you're acting," she commented sweetly.

"All right, wear the damned thing, then. But don't say I didn't warn you," he capitulated ungraciously. He eyed her grimly. "You plan on taking a shawl or something, I hope? You wouldn't want to get pneumonia."

Kacie giggled at his dire expression and saucily swished her hips as she headed for her room to collect her wrap and her bag. "I trust you to keep me warm," she teased daringly, riding high from his blatant proprietary display.

He honored her with a grunt of annoyance and a muttered epithet on the peculiarities of women, which she ignored.

Fortunately for her, Jake wasn't the type of man to spoil an evening nursing a grievance. Apparently, having said his piece, he preferred to ignore the whole episode: that is, if Kacie discounted the possessive hold he had on her arm as they entered the magnificent three-story mansion ablaze with lights.

Once inside, Kacie was more than grateful for his reassuring presence. Never had she seen so many elaborately gowned women in her life, not to mention their formally attired escorts. There was no sign of their host as Kacie handed her shawl and bag to the maid stationed by the foyer for just that purpose.

"Abbey wasn't exaggerating," Kacie observed in a whisper.

She gazed around the huge room where the other guests were gathered. At the far end she saw long windows thrown open, leading to a wide stone terrace dotted with white-draped tables. To her right, beautifully carved doors were parted to allow free access to the ballroom, where a band was playing.

"Let's circulate," Jake suggested, drawing her into the festive group. "Mark's bound to be here somewhere."

"Surely these aren't all stockholders?" Kacie voiced in surprise.

"No," Jake agreed absently, nodding in response to

the greetings called out to them as they passed. "There he is."

Kacie followed Jake's gaze to the tall, silver-haired man in his late fifties holding court over a small cluster of graying men.

"Jake, so glad you could make it," Mark Stratton greeted them as he moved away from the group. "And this must be Kacie."

Kacie smiled politely and extended her hand.

"You look surprised, my dear," Mark observed in a charming drawl. "If I hadn't known you from Abbey's description, I certainly would have from Jake's."

Kacie glanced up at Jake, finding his eyes fastened on her with a possessiveness in the ebony depths that made her skin glow with warmth.

Jake's arm around her waist tightened briefly before he gave his attention to his host. "Did I lie?" he asked with a grin of masculine satisfaction.

Mark's shrewd dark eyes observed the intimate byplay between his friend and the raven-haired Kacie.

"No," he replied honestly. "That brings me to another question."

Jake's eyebrow raised at the almost hesitant tone.

"Who is this Bill whom Abbey quotes at every opportunity?"

Jake chuckled. "Does she really? Good for her."

Mark looked anything but pleased at Jake's response, Kacie decided as she stood in the circle of Jake's arm, watching the older man's face.

"Well?" Mark prompted.

Jake shrugged his massive shoulders in a dismissive gesture. "He's my home-office VP and a friend." There was a subtle emphasis of warning on the last word.

"You approve?" Mark's gaze was intent on Jake's expression.

Immediately Jake nodded. "I do. You won't find a better man than Bill."

"I thought I had," Mark replied dryly, "but it seems I was wrong."

Kacie felt her color rise as Mark's eyes settled significantly on her.

"You were," Jake affirmed flatly.

Mark smiled apologetically. "You can't blame an old man for trying."

"If you're going to play that lonely-uncle-needing-a-family-to-help-him-through-his-declining-years charade again, Mark, we're leaving," Jake threatened with a chuckle. "Come on, Kacie."

With a smile at their unrepentant host, Kacie allowed Jake to guide her toward the ballroom.

"I'm tired of talking. I just want to hold you in my arms," he whispered softly, swinging her onto the dance floor.

With a contented sigh, Kacie flowed into his embrace, her body brushing lightly against his. Because they were not alone, she was denied the pleasure of molding herself to Jake's large frame as she ached to do. The melodic strains of a soft waltz filled her ears, heightening her physical awareness of the man who held her. She took a deep breath, striving for control over her clamoring emotions. What she needed was a distraction. Something to take her mind off Jake's silent assault on her senses.

"Mark is nothing like I pictured from your and Abbey's descriptions," she remarked with only a trace of breathlessness betraying her slipping control.

"Don't let that easy manner fool you," Jake commented quietly, his arm tightening around her bare back to steer her away from another couple. He made no move to ease the closeness between them when they were safely clear.

She shook her head slightly. "I didn't mean that. I meant he doesn't seem the type of man to push Abbey into a fake..." She stopped, groping for the word to describe the odd arrangement between Abbey and Jake.

Jake completed her sentence for her: "Relationship with me?"

"Yes." She stared up at him questioningly.

"Jealous?" There was a hopeful gleam in his eyes that Kacie didn't miss.

For a second she debated denying it. "A little," she admitted.

"Good." Jake grinned, hauling her even closer.

"Jake, I can't breathe," she objected as his chin settled against her temple. She wiggled carefully, trying to ease away. Much as she loved the warm haven he created around her, she was conscious of the people nearby. Luckily the music chose that moment to end.

With a reluctant sigh, Jake let her move out of his arms, although he kept one hand firmly curved about her hip, effectively anchoring her to his side.

"Would you like something to drink?" he asked solicitously. Not waiting for an answer, he propelled her forward in the direction of the bar set up by the terrace windows.

"What I'd like is an explanation," she grumbled, catching sight of the raised eyebrows their tandem progress produced. Jake was giving a good imitation of a dog guarding his favorite bone, the practical Kacie decided with an inward grimace. *Or a man so much in love, he doesn't care who knows it,* the more imaginative Irish replied with a clearly visible satisfied smile.

"What are you grinning about?" Jake passed her a chilled glass of white wine before picking up his own bourbon and water.

"Oh, nothing," Kacie replied lightly, suddenly enjoying Jake's exclusive attention. Why should she care that there were people looking if he didn't? "Could we go out on the terrace?"

Jake looked around before nodding agreeably. "It is sort of hot in here."

"And crowded," Kacie added, stepping through the door with Jake at her side.

The soft evening breeze stirring the leaves of the trees felt deliciously cooling against her skin. Jake led her away from the open windows toward the shadowed tables set up on the outer edges of the stone landing. The noise and music from the party faded to a low drone in the background.

Kacie took the seat Jake pulled out from the small oval table overlooking the gardens. "Mark has a beautiful home," she acknowledged softly in the quiet surrounding.

"Would you—" Jake began.

"Oh, there you are, sir."

Both Kacie and Jake looked around, startled by the cheerful intrusion of a red-coated waiter.

"Yes?" Jake prompted.

"Mr. Stratton asked if you could spare him five minutes in the library, sir. It's important."

"Now?" The man nodded.

Jake glanced to Kacie's worried face. "Don't look so perturbed. It concerns the stocks I told you about. Will you be all right, or do you want to go back inside?"

Kacie shook her head. "I'd rather wait here."

After brushing a quick, appreciative kiss across her parted lips, he rose. "Okay, I won't be long."

She watched him stride away, feeling surprisingly bereft without his presence.

"Well, well, well. As I live and breathe. Look who I found in the garden."

Kacie started at the mocking voice coming from the shadowy fringe of the garden. She stared intently into the darkness, recognizing the voice. "John?"

"None other." John Lockhart sauntered onto the lighted terrace.

Sheer surprise at his impolite attitude drove every coherent thought from Kacie's mind. "What are you doing here?" she asked stupidly.

"Clearing my head from too much noise," he replied, pulling out the chair Jake had just vacated.

Finding her wits, Kacie stared at him coolly, not liking his tone at all. "That place is taken."

"So I see." Pointedly ignoring her irritation, he sat down anyway. Leaning back, he studied her figure with narrowed eyes. "So you and the boss are a pair, are you?"

Kacie stared back at her accuser, astounded at the change in him. Where was the pleasant man she had worked with? She eyed him suspiciously, wondering if he had had too much to drink or whether he was still feeling piqued over their aborted date.

"Look, what is it you want from me?" she demanded, her temper rising at the assessing glitter in his eyes.

John smiled, showing too-perfect white teeth. "A kiss?" he suggested with a unfamiliar caressing murmur.

It triggered nothing but disgust in her—and an urgent

desire for Jake's reassuring presence. "John, if you'll excuse me," she began, hoping to escape the distasteful scene she felt was coming.

"Don't go." John reached out to trail a finger across Kacie's arm. "I remember how much fun we had, don't you?"

"No." Kacie pulled away abruptly and pushed back her chair. Rising to her feet, she glared across at his seemingly relaxed figure. "I don't know what's wrong with you, but I'm leaving."

She turned, intending to put as much distance between them as possible. Where was Jake when she needed him, she wondered angrily.

John's arm snaked around her waist, effectively halting her in her tracks. She felt the heated brush of his breath across her bare neck. The smell of liquor confirmed her suspicions. "Where are you going, honey?"

She struggled against the iron grip holding her prisoner. "Let me go, John!" she demanded, suddenly conscious of how isolated they were from the rest of the party.

He turned her around in his arms, effectively stilling her attempts to elude him. "Gimme a kiss and I will," he slurred.

Seeing the intent in his eyes, Kacie pushed her hands against his shoulders, leaning back as far as she could to avoid his descending mouth. Turning her head away, she suddenly spied Jake's massive form striding purposefully toward them. She barely had time to register the pure rage blazing in his eyes. John was torn free as Jake grabbed his shoulder and spun him away like a bothersome fly.

John crashed into the table with a grunt of pain, then

drunkenly slithered to the stone floor, landing in a heap.

Kacie was trembling with relief as she turned her eyes to her avenging guardian, but the fury in Jake's expression chased shivers of fear through her. Surely he didn't think she'd been cooperating!

"What the hell was he doing here?" Jake bit out tersely, jerking a thumb in the direction of his fallen foe. His eyes never left Kacie's white face.

"He came just after you left. He wouldn't go, or let me leave, either," she whispered shakily. Her lashes fell shut as the ebony gaze flamed at her explanation of John's advances.

Steellike fingers imprisoned her limp wrist. "We're leaving."

Kacie's eyes flew open at the gritted announcement. "Jake, I can—"

Paying no attention to her attempt to explain, Jake started for the garden path, hauling her behind him by her manacled wrist.

She stumbled breathlessly behind him, unable to free her arm or force him to slow down. Between the stone path and her very high heels, she didn't have a chance at keeping up with his long-legged strides.

"Please, Jake," she whimpered as she tripped awkwardly over the concrete edge of the drive and cannoned into Jake as he stopped to search the parking area for his car.

"Just be quiet, Kacie. Now!" The last was a low growl of warning meant to be obeyed.

Panting, she leaned heavily against his side, grateful for the empty darkness concealing their progress.

Walking was easier now as Jake pulled her down the end row to his waiting car. Without a word, he pushed her inside and slammed the door. There was controlled violence in him as he swung the powerful machine out between the iron gates of Mark's estate and onto the road back to the city.

Kacie sat huddled in her seat. For the first time in her relationship with Jake she knew fear. She couldn't understand the rage in him. She hadn't missed the sheer brute strength of his reaction to John's handling of her. John wasn't a small man by any means, yet Jake had tossed him aside as if he were a lightweight.

"Get out." With the door open, Jake stood at her side of the car.

Kacie flinched at the harsh command. Looking around, she dazedly realized they were in Jake's penthouse garage. "Jake, please let me ex—"

"Do you want me to carry you?" Jake leaned toward her threateningly.

Nervously, she swallowed the lump in her throat at his angry face. "No," she replied, sliding out of her seat.

Thankfully, this time Jake contented himself with escorting her toward the elevator.

Like a jailer taking a prisoner to the firing squad, Kacie thought with morbid humor. The ride to the top floor took place in total silence.

For Kacie, it provided a badly needed breathing space. Her shock and fright from John's behavior were finally subsiding. Under Jake's unswerving black gaze, she found her temper rising. *How dare he treat her like this!*

The doors silently slid open.

Suddenly Kacie wanted the privacy of Jake's apartment as much as he obviously did. She had a thing or two she wanted to tell the mighty giant. She'd fry his damned ears, she fumed in self-righteous anger as she stalked ahead of Jake into the luxurious living room.

"Now suppose you tell me what the hell was going on in that garden, Kacie Daniels. And it'd better be good," Jake commanded, slamming the door with an angry bang.

Kacie whirled around, facing his towering form with less than a foot of space between them.

"Tell you! Tell you!" she hissed, her eyes shooting sparks of blue fire. "I tried to tell you, and you told me to shut up!"

Jake's jaw clenched as he glared across at her. "That was then. This is now." He waited, his arms folded across his chest. "Well?"

The barely leashed temper in his prompting abruptly convinced Kacie to give him what he wanted.

"John saw me in the garden, and he invited himself over."

"Why didn't you tell him to get lost?" Jake cut in.

"I did," she snapped back indignantly. "Since he wouldn't leave, I decided to go and look for you."

Jake stepped across the tiny gulf separating them and grabbed her shoulders. "Was that before or after he kissed you?" he growled furiously.

Kacie put her hands against his chest and pushed with all her strength. "Let me go, damn you. Do I have to be attacked twice in the same night?" she shouted with a fury to match his own.

"Attacked!" Jake shook her. "There was damned little attacking going on from where I was standing."

Enraged by his failure to believe her, Kacie decided to hit back. "What difference does it make to you, anyway? After all, I'm only your blasted mistress...not even that, really. A stupid bed partner."

A flush darkening his jaw, he released her as though he had been slapped.

"Bed partner! You crazy Irish witch. I love you!" Clearly stunned by his own words, he stood staring blankly into Kacie's furious expression.

"'Irish witch'! You pig-headed, blind Yankee!" Kacie's mouth snapped shut as the full meaning of Jake's words sank into her brain. "Love me? You love me?" she echoed in an amazed whisper, her eyes glued to Jake's.

"Yes," he admitted in a quieter tone. He ran a hand across the back of his neck in a weary gesture and took off his jacket. "I need a drink."

Kacie stared at him. He didn't remotely resemble a man in the throes of love. Irritable, tired, even a little angry—but certainly not happy.

"Do you want one?" Jake gestured toward the extensive liquor selection.

Shaking her head, Kacie sank into the nearest chair. Bewildered at his attitude, she watched Jake pour himself a neat bourbon and down it.

"When?" she finally asked when Jake showed no signs of breaking the silence that had fallen between them.

Jake took his time answering, refilling his glass and adding a splash of water to his liquor. He took a seat across from her.

"Tonight."

Kacie nodded, suddenly understanding his overreaction to the embrace he'd witnessed. He had been wildly, incredibly jealous.

"I was so angry." Jake stared at the amber liquid in his glass. "I've never been as close to hurting, really hurting, someone as I was when I saw you in that creep's arms." He raised his eyes, spearing her with a possessive look. "You're mine. And *nobody,* not even you, is going to take you away from me." The deep growl was raw with the force of awakened emotions.

Something primitive in Kacie thrilled to the sheer male determination. She had almost given up hope of believing Jake could ever come to love her as she loved him. Instinct guided her to approach his seated figure and she perched on the arm of his chair, the need to comfort and reassure him of her love paramount as she took the half-full glass from his hands. "John means nothing to me. You know that. It's you I love." Her voice was rich with the force of her own emotions.

Jake raised his head to stare into her eyes. Hesitantly, almost as if he were afraid to reach out for her, he lifted his hand and gently brushed her cheek.

Kacie read the aching hunger in his eyes and responded. Her giant, her strong mighty giant, needed her. She nuzzled her face into his palm, her eyes never leaving his. "I love you, Jake, so much," she breathed in a throbbing whisper.

"Do you, Irish? Be sure, little witch," he murmured, drawing her into his lap. "It's taken me a long time to find you. I don't think I could bear to let you go now that you're really mine."

Twining her arms around his neck, Kacie cradled his head against her breast. His sigh rippled across the fragile velvet. His arms tightened around her until she felt each breath he took as her own.

"Marry me, little witch." It was a command laced with pleading. "Fill my nights and my days with your love." He lifted his head.

"Are you sure that's what you want?" she asked, needing her own form of reassurance. "You don't have to, you know."

"Yes, I do. I want you chained to me with every link God and man ever invented," he insisted. "No more nights like tonight." He ran his hand caressingly across her bare back, then frowned. "Or any more dresses like this one."

Kacie buried her face in the column of his throat to hide the smile his annoyed comment provoked. "You know it's a beautiful gown," she murmured teasingly, secretly delighted with his possessive attitude. Hadn't she felt equally upset about the supposed relationship between him and Abbey?

"It is," he agreed with deceptive innocence. "You can wear it for our wedding-night dinner."

"Oh?" She prompted curiously.

He nodded, his eyes glinting devilishly. "Uh huh. Think of all the time I'll save getting you out of it."

Giggling, Kacie stuck out her tongue. "I haven't said I'll marry you yet," she reminded him, daring to tease him as he had so often baited her.

"Jake!" she squealed as he stood up in one smooth motion with her in his arms. "What are you doing?"

"Combining a bit of business with a bit of pleasure," he explained in a low growl as he strode across the room and kicked open the bedroom door.

"What are you talking about?" she demanded as he came to a stop beside the massive king-size bed she remembered so well.

"I, my wife-to-be"—he paused to kiss her parted lips, a quick teasing caress that left Kacie hungry for more— "am going to get down to the business of convincing you how necessary it is for us to get married. But"—he paused again to lower her to her feet—"before that, I'm going to have the pleasure of uncovering the real you this thing . . ."—experienced hands eased both shoulders of her gown down her bare arms until the fabric slipped soundlessly to the floor—" . . . almost conceals," he finished on a husky note when she stood revealed before him in a pool of blue velvet. The soft glow of the single bedroom lamp glistened on her pearly skin.

"I might need convincing," Kacie dared provocatively.

The sweep of Jake's proprietary gaze over her body set alight the smoldering embers of desire waiting for his flaming touch. She swayed toward him in surrender, all thoughts of teasing gone.

Accepting both her voiced challenge and her physical concession, Jake took her in his arms. He lowered her gently to the waiting bed, covering her mouth with his. Her lips flowered open at his demand, and he drank deeply of the sweet nectar of passion. He raised his head to gaze upon her face, flushed pink by the potency of his kiss.

"Just remember—I'm still your boss, and I give the orders," he warned in a voice raw with emotion.

Unable to deny the desire Jake had ignited, Kacie reached for him, pulling him down until his body pressed the warm softness of her own.

"Yes, Jake," she murmured appeasingly before reaching hungrily for his lips so tantalizingly close.

WHAT READERS SAY ABOUT
SECOND CHANCE AT LOVE BOOKS

"Your books are the greatest!"
    —*M. N., Carteret, New Jersey**

"I have been reading romance novels for quite some time,
but the SECOND CHANCE AT LOVE books are the
most enjoyable."
    —*P. R., Vicksburg, Mississippi**

"I enjoy SECOND CHANCE [AT LOVE] more than any
books that I have read and I do read a lot."
    —*J. R., Gretna, Louisiana**

"I really think your books are exceptional...I read
Harlequin and Silhouette and although I still like them,
I'll buy your books over theirs. SECOND CHANCE [AT
LOVE] is more interesting and holds your attention and
imagination with a better story line..."
    —*J. W., Flagstaff, Arizona**

"I've read many romances, but yours take the 'cake'!"
    —*D. H., Bloomsburg, Pennsylvania**

"Have waited ten years for *good* romance books. Now I
have them."
    —*M. P., Jacksonville, Florida**

*Names and addresses available upon request